Powerful Prayers for All Seasons
New Testament Edition

Teron V. Gaddis

Powerful Prayers New Testament Edition
Copyright © 2021 by Pastor G Ministries

All Scripture quotations unless otherwise indicated are taken from The Holy Bible, English Standard Version.

Gaddis, Teron V., 1964-

Senior Editor: Ramona Y. Simmons

Edited by: Dr. Lisa Smith-Jack, Jamila M. Woodard

Cover design: Paula McDade

Author photo: Omar Lampley

ISBN-13: 978-0-578-84474-9
(Pastor G Ministries)
First Printing 2021

Printed in the United States of America

DEDICATION

To the families of those who lost their lives to the 2020 global pandemic, especially our Pastors. Well done thy good and faithful servants. May this book remind you to never stop praying. God has a prayer for every one of our needs.

"Pastor Teron V. Gaddis in Powerful Prayers for All Seasons teaches us that there is a specific prayer for each season we experience. This book helps the believer to explore ways to overcome through prayer in whatever season you are experiencing."
Rev. Antonio D. Anderson, M.Div., Senior Pastor
Mount Tabor Baptist Church of Germantown

"I have discovered that far too many who consider themselves believers in Jesus Christ are deficient in having a natural organic prayer life. We must practice robust and consistent prayer to God and not just when we get into a troublesome situation. I'm grateful for the example set by Pastor Teron Gaddis is leading us into said consistent communication with our Lord."
Pastor Lance A. Mann, Sr. Pastor
Solid Rock Baptist Church, Paris TX

"The only thing that stands between you and an answer prayer is faith in God."
Rev. C.J. Lubin, Senior Pastor of True Vine Ministries Spencer, OK

"As I reflect on my recent journey, I made the decision to not hit the "panic' button; instead I made a conscious choice to hit the "prayer' button. It is because of answered prayers, each day moving forward; I commit to hitting the "praise' button. It happens after prayer. Thanks Pastor Gaddis!"
Rev. E. Jennings Tyson, Pastor
New Hope Baptist Church, Oklahoma City, Ok

"Personal prayer is an intricate element in the spiritual growth of every believer. This is because you can't become spiritually mature until you accept your unchanging need for God's help."
Romell Williams, Lead Pastor
The Progression Church, Chicago, IL

ACKNOWLEDGMENTS

Sincerely grateful to God Almighty who gave me the strength to write during a global pandemic. He has burdened my heart with prayer. I am eternally grateful to my wife, Janice of thirty-four years, who has prayed continuously for me and extended grace while my primary focus was pastoring and writing. Through 29 years of ministry she is still by my side. I must also thank my writing team: Ramona Y. Simmons (Senior Editor) who keeps me on schedule as much as she can and helps make my vision a reality. Dr. Lisa Jack and Jamila M. Woodard (Editors), who still accept my drafts with impossible deadlines attached to them. I also want to thank Paula McDade for the fabulous cover. This would not be possible without them.

1 A PRAYER FOR RIGHT PRIORITIES

---

[25] *"Therefore I tell you, do not be anxious about your life, what you will eat or what you will drink, nor about your body, what you will put on. Is not life more than food, and the body more than clothing?* [26] *Look at the birds of the air: they neither sow nor reap nor gather into barns, and yet your heavenly Father feeds them. Are you not of more value than they?* [27] *And which of you by being anxious can add a single hour to his span of life?* [28] *And why are you anxious about clothing? Consider the lilies of the field, how they grow: they neither toil nor spin,* [29] *yet I tell you, even Solomon in all his glory was not arrayed like one of these.* [30] *But if God so clothes the grass of the field, which today is alive and tomorrow is thrown into the oven, will he not much more clothe you, O you of little faith?* [31] *Therefore do not be anxious, saying, 'What shall we eat?' or 'What shall we drink?' or 'What shall we wear?'* [32] *For the Gentiles seek after all these things, and your heavenly Father knows that you need them all.* [33] *But seek first the kingdom of God and his righteousness, and all these things will be added to you.* [34] *"Therefore do not be anxious about tomorrow, for tomorrow will be anxious for itself. Sufficient for the day is its own trouble." Matthew 6:25-34*

American Jazz musician Bobby McFerrin released a song in 1988. It became America's first acapella and reggae song to reach number-one on the Billboard Hot 100 for more than two weeks. This song sounded unlike anything else on the radio. I am sure once you read the lyrics it will bring back memories.

Here's a little song I wrote

You might want to sing it note for note

Don't worry, be happy

In every life we have some trouble

But when you worry you make it double

Don't worry, be happy

Worry is one of the most destructive habits people get caught in. It has definitely been one of my biggest issues and I know I am not alone.

"Worry often gives a small thing a big shadow." – **Swedish Proverb**

"Worry is like a rocking chair: it gives you something to do but never gets you anywhere"
– **Erma Bombeck**

"There is a great difference between worry and concern. A worried person sees a problem, and a concerned person solves a problem."
– **Harold Stephen**

First, **worry is distrusting the wisdom of God**. When we worry, we are saying, *"God, I do not believe you can handle this all by Yourself."*

Secondly, **worry is denying the Word of God**. Worry tells God we do not believe He will keep His Word. When we worry, we live at the expense of our disturbance and the expense of God's displeasure.

Is there an antidote for worry? Is there a way, not only to deal with worry, but also destroy worry? Can we, as believers, live our lives worry-free?

The answer to all the aforementioned questions is yes! Our Lord and Savior Jesus Christ explained how in the greatest sermon ever preached, the Sermon on the Mount. Jesus tells us there is a way we do not have to live stressed, strung out and twisted up with worry." We must **TRUST** the **FATHER'S CARE**!

Jesus says in **Matthew 6:25**, ***"Therefore I tell you, do not be anxious about your life, what you will eat or what you will drink, nor about your body, what you will put on. Is not life more than food, and the body more than clothing?***

Jesus is teaching us that we will not worry if we remember to trust God the Father. The phrase, **"*do not be anxious,*"** simply means, ***"do not worry."*** Jesus is not advocating going through life with your head stuck in the sand oblivious. Absolutely not! He is saying there is no need to worry because He cares for us.

The master teacher not only commands us not to worry, but He gives reasons why we are not to worry. This should give all believers a reason to rejoice. Why? Because the reason we should not worry has nothing to do with our ability and everything to do with God's ability to take care of us.

To further explain this thought, Jesus refers to two objects He created. The birds in the air **(v.6:26)** and the lilies of the field **(v.6:27)**. Let us look deeper into the analogy Jesus used. The birds of the air do not plant or harvest, nor do they maintain a storehouse. How are they cared for? Our Heavenly Father feeds them. One of those tiny birds cannot fall to the ground without God taking notice. He is asking you today, "Are you not of more value than they?"

Of course, the answer to God's question is yes! We are much more valuable than the birds of the air. God is assuring us to worry about this matter is foolish. Jesus says in **Matthew 6:27**, "And which of you by being anxious can add a single hour to his span of life?

Matthew 6:28 says, **"And why are you anxious about clothing? Consider the lilies of the field, how they grow: they neither toil nor spin."** Jesus says the lilies do not strain or strive to produce growth and beauty. They do not worry about how big they grow, how fast they grow, or even where they grow. They do what God created them to do, grow!

Verse 29 says, "**yet I tell you, even Solomon in all his glory was not arrayed like one of these."** It is estimated that if Solomon's temple was built today using all of the same furnishings of the Old

Testament, it would be worth more than $40 billion. Yet, Jesus says that does not even compare to the lilies of the field.

Read verse 30 aloud.

"But if God so clothes the grass of the field, which today is alive and tomorrow is thrown into the oven, will he not much more clothe you, O you of little faith?"

The ultimate indictment here is worry is the opposite of faith.

Do not miss the lesson the Master is teaching. Worry looks to what we can do, while faith looks to what God can do. Worry discounts, denies and distrusts the promises of God. However, faith believes and behaves according to the promises of God. Jesus is saying when we worry, we are guilty of faithlessness.

> *Greek scholar, Kenneth Wuest said, "God commands us to stop worrying about even one thing. We commit sin when we worry. We do not trust God when we worry. We do not receive answers to prayer when we worry, because we are not trusting God."*

Read verse 32. **"For the Gentiles seek after all these things."** You see, when we who know God worry, we are acting like pagan Gentiles who do not know God. Let me restate the obvious. It is foolish and faithless to worry because our **"heavenly Father knows that you need them all."**

The Bible repeatedly reminds you and me to…

- *fret not, because God loves us.*

- *faint not, because God holds us.*

- *and, fear not, because God keeps us.*

Jesus further admonishes us to, **"seek first the kingdom of God and his righteousness, and all these things will be added to you" (v.6:33).** This is one of the most important verses of scripture in the Bible. It is insightful and instructional. This verse has a foundational premise, a rational principle, and an eternal promise.

The context of the verse is worry. The word **'seek'** is used in the imperative tense, which speaks of continually seeking. It denotes a determined, deliberate and diligent pursuit of the things of God. Every day you and I are blessed and highly favored to live free. We are to put God first in every aspect of our lives.

Allow me to give you the Gaddis translation.

Jesus is saying God must come before our family, finances and future.

Jesus is saying God must be first in all our relationships, recreation and revenue.

Jesus is saying God must have priority over our ambitions, appetites and aspirations.

Jesus is saying God must come before our cash flow, credit score, clothes' closet and creature comforts.

God will not play second fiddle to anyone or anything. He will not be Lord at all unless He is Lord of all. He desires not just to be present in our lives. His desire is to be President. He is not satisfied with being our co-pilot; He wants to be our Pilot.

What is the result of a life lived under the Lordship of Jesus Christ? What happens when God is given His rightful place? Jesus says that, **"all these things will be added to you."** What *'things'* is Jesus referring to? He is referring to the basic necessities of life, food, clothing, shelter and finances. When we do not worry and instead put Him first, He will see to it that **"all these things will be added to you."**

Let me remind you once again this promise of provision is only for those who **"seek first the kingdom of God and his righteousness."** If a person does not enthrone, embrace or establish Jesus Christ as the Lord of their life, they cannot lay claim to the promise of God's provision for their every need.

Will you allow me just this moment to give you a very important announcement? A life not committed to Christ with Him as Lord, and not seeking Him is headed for a life filled with worry, confusion and turmoil.

If serving God is an option…

If you come to church, Sunday school and choir practice only when you feel like coming…

If you give only when it is convenient, and tip rather than tithe…

If you follow God when the chips are down, but forsake God when the chips are up…

If you crave what you want more than what God wants…

…then you cannot lay your head down tonight knowing God will take care of you.

Read Matthew 6:34 aloud. **"Therefore do not be anxious about tomorrow, for tomorrow will be anxious for itself. Sufficient for the day is its own trouble."** Jesus reminds us that our Heavenly Father is in perfect control of everyday life. Therefore, when you and I accept His control it alleviates worry and we enjoy the lives He has purposed, planned and prepared for us.

Jesus is saying not only should you and I not worry about today, but we should not worry about tomorrow as well. The things of tomorrow will take care of themselves and our worrying about them will not change them.

I heard a preacher say we have less time on earth as we did yesterday. In other words, the Bible never promises us we will live to see tomorrow. Thus, to worry about something that may never come is preposterous, because tomorrow already has enough problems without compounding the problems with our worry.

Consider this idea, when we turn to God and bring Him our problems and pressures; our burdens and battles; our troubles and trials; our concerns and cares; and our difficulties and decisions, life becomes more simplified and more satisfied. We can rest in the Lord, rely on the Lord and let Him worry about the things which worry us. If the year 2020 has taught you and me anything, it has been we need to do our part and let God do His part in everything.

If the economy shuts down, bring it to Jesus and let Him worry about it.

If the doors of the business close, bring it to Jesus and let Him worry about it.

If the love of your life walks out, bring it to Jesus and let Him worry about it.

If there are more bills than money at the end of the month, bring it to Jesus and let Him worry about it.

He has promised that if we trust in His care for us, obey His command and accept His control He will protect us, preserve us and provide for us. So, what are you worried about? Enjoy the simplified and satisfied life He has made available.

Horatio Spafford was born in 1828. He became a baron in the real estate industry and a man of great wealth. Yet, through all of his success he never forgot the hand of God which had blessed Him and he gave God all the glory. He lived in Chicago and in the midst of the Great Chicago fire of 1871, Horatio Spafford lost it all. He lost his business and his only son. Suddenly, he felt the clouds of circumstance and doubt surrounding him. His wife became almost to the point of depression over their loss of everything, so he put her and their 4 daughters on a ship headed for England. Spafford stayed behind in

Chicago to handle a few business matters and would set out to meet them, in England, in 2 weeks.

Somewhere near the middle of his family's voyage the ship was stuck by an English vessel and sank in 12 minutes. All 4 of Spafford's daughters, were among the 226 who drowned. Only his wife survived and when she arrived in Cardiff, Wales, she sent him a telegram that read, "Saved Alone!" Spafford jumped on board the next ship headed to England to be at the side of his wife. He sent word to the captain that when they arrived at the place where his daughters had drowned to come get him in his cabin and walk him to the deck. Finally, they came to the spot where the boat sank.

The captain sent for Spafford and he walked up to the deck overlooking the icy waters of the North Atlantic, the very spot where his 4 daughters had perished. As he stood there his mind was filled with doubt, confusion and turmoil. He had lost his business, his son and now his 4 daughters. However, in the midst of the darkest hour of his life an overwhelming sense of peace flooded his soul. He knew as never before; God was in control and would see him through. Horatio Spafford went back to the cabin, sat down at his desk and penned these words to paper:

When peace like a river
Attendeth my way.
When sorrows like sea billows roll.

Whatever my lot,

Thou hast taught me to say,

It is well; it is well, with my soul.

Tho Satan should buffet,

Tho trials should come;

Let this blest assurance control,

That Christ hath regarded my helpless estate

And shed His own blood for my soul.

I say to you if you will commit your life to the Lord Jesus Christ and trust His care, obey His command and accept His control; you can enjoy a simplified and satisfied life, and say with Spafford, come what may 'it is well with my soul.' You don't have to live all stressed with nowhere to go!

2 A PRAYER OF REST FOR THE WEARY

25 At that time Jesus declared, "I thank you, Father, Lord of heaven and earth, that you have hidden these things from the wise and understanding and revealed them to little children; 26 yes, Father, for such was your gracious will. 27 All things have been handed over to me by my Father, and no one knows the Son except the Father, and no one knows the Father except the Son and anyone to whom the Son chooses to reveal him. 28 Come to me, all who labor and are heavy laden, and I will give you rest. 29 Take my yoke upon you, and learn from me, for I am gentle and lowly in heart, and you will find rest for your souls. 30 For my yoke is easy, and my burden is light."
Matthew 11:25-30

The COVID-19 pandemic has altered every aspect of American life. Health, work, education and exercise are just a few of the things altered. According to the American Psychological Association (APA), it is predicted the negative mental health effects of the coronavirus will be serious and long-lasting. To better understand how individuals are coping with the extreme stress of this crisis, the once annual poll has been converted to a monthly analysis of stressors and stress levels for people. Taking a monthly "pulse" to understand how individuals are processing these extreme events will help health leaders and policymakers better align advice and resources to address these evolving mental health needs.

The Harris Poll conducted this survey on behalf of APA from April 24 to May 4, 2020; the online survey included 3,013 adults age 18+ who reside in the United States.

- Covid-19 stress is taking a toll on United State parents.
- Government response to covid-19 is a significant source of stress for nearly 7 in 10 adults.
- Stress related to economy and work increase significantly during the pandemic compared with 2019.
- People of color more likely to report higher stress related to covid-19.

The second poll, conducted from May 21 to June 3, 2020, among 3,013 adults ages 18 and older who reside in the United States revealed these results.

- Most Americans say the future of our nation is a significant source of stress.

- Black Americans report discrimination is a significant stressor.

- Government response to coronavirus is a significant stressor for majority of Americans.

- Parents stress about the long-term impacts of covid-19 on children.

Volume 3 the Harris poll conducted this survey on behalf of APA from June 23 to July 6, 2020; the online survey included 3,010 adults age 18+ who reside in the United States.

- Majority of democrats and republicans report covid-19 prevention measures are reassuring; cite current stressors.

- American stress levels related to the coronavirus pandemic hold steady, but feelings of frustration, fear and anger are rising.

- As covid-19 moves west and south, so do higher stress levels about the virus.

- Certain aspects of racial injustice spur stress and action.

It is one thing to experience physical fatigue, but I believe there are other kinds of fatigue more debilitating. There is mental fatigue, emotional fatigue, and there is spiritual fatigue. The remedy for physical fatigue is sleep, but the only remedy for the other kind of fatigues are rest. There is a difference. You can go to a drugstore and buy something to put you to sleep, but you can't buy anything that will give you the kind of rest you need for your heart, soul and mind.

You get so tired and weary of fighting for your marriage. You just give up and check out.

You get so weary of the financial pressures of life you just let bills go unpaid and don't answer the phone when the collectors call.

Some people just get so tired and weary of life they just end their life.

A lot of us are messed up because we are stressed out.

We have gone about as far as we can go.

We have carried about as much as we can bear.

We have taken about as much as we can stand.

Today, we are going to look at God's remedy for the weary. All of us can identify with feeling overloaded, overworked, overcommitted, overextended, and overanxious. Have you ever felt like your emotional tank is empty and you are running on fumes? Maybe you are at this place right now.

Do you know what it means to be overwhelmed? It is a symptom of what some call "deficit living." Overwhelmed people live in deficit.

It could be an emotional, relational, or spiritual deficit. Do you remember when you opened your first bank account and ordered your first box of checks? For my young readers a check is the piece of paper you saw your grandparents write on and give to the cashier or put in the offering plate at church. When your checks arrived in the mail, you felt so grown-up. What is one of the very first lessons you learned about writing checks? You must keep track of your balance or your account will be overdrawn. An overdrawn check account is an automatic stressor.

Just like a checking account, it is possible to get overdrawn in life. When you get overwhelmed you find yourself living in deficit. You have run out of the emotional currency needed to cover the bank account of life.

People who are overwhelmed with stress need to add words that begin with the prefix, "re". They are words like restore, relax, revive, replenish, renew, and refresh. Jesus knows exactly what your problem is, and even better, He has the perfect solution. No matter what He **knows** exactly what you are going **through**, exactly how you **feel**, and exactly how to **get through** it.

God has never known…

- *A problem that's too big to solve*
- *A circumstance that's too difficult to change*

- *A night that's too dark to brighten*

- *A heart that's too broken to bless*

- *A question that's too hard to answer*

- *A joy that's too lost to restore*

- *A crisis that's too critical to confront*

Eugene Peterson translates **Matthew 11:28** like this. **"Are you tired? Worn out? Burned out on religion? Come to me. Get away with me and you'll recover your life. I'll show you how to take a real rest. Walk with me and work with me-watch how I do it. Learn the unforced rhythms of grace. I won't lay anything heavy or ill-fitting on you. Keep company with me and you'll learn to live freely and lightly.'"**

The word *"labor"* is a very interesting word. It is used to describe the exhaustion of a soldier in battle or a messenger who had run many miles to deliver his message. It means *"working to the point of absolute exhaustion."* It is also used to describe a ship loaded with so much weight it is sinking or an animal that has so much weight it is collapsing. In other words, Jesus is talking to people so tired they cannot go any further and are so burdened they cannot take anymore. He is talking about people who need to stop and rest.

If you are tired of living on edge, tired of going through the motions, tired of rocking in a chair, going nowhere, then Jesus has a word for you. Jesus helps us using three simple words, come, take and learn. If life has you down and you are ready to wave the white flag, let me give you the simple advice from the one who can handle anything.

First, Jesus says, **[28] Come to me, all who labor and are heavy laden, and I will give you rest.** Notice Jesus did not say, "Come to church." He said, **"Come to me."** In other words, take all the necessary and unnecessary stuff, the burdens weighing you down and set them down and come into the presence of Jesus. This is where a lot of people miss the mark, because so many people who are tired, burned out, frustrated, and stressed out cannot find any rest, because they keep looking for it in the wrong places. People try to do so many things to get rid of their stress, but rest doesn't come. We try to drink, smoke, and sex our problems away.

Some people scramble, burning the midnight oil trying to get further ahead and higher up the ladder. They do all they know to do, the best way they know to do it, but still no rest. A lot of people think money is the answer. They say, "If I just had enough money all my problems would be solved. Money would allow me to do everything I want to do and buy everything I need to buy." It takes some people a lifetime to realize not only is money not the answer, but often times it is the problem.

Money can buy a lot of good things in life. It can't, however, buy the best things in life. It can buy a house, but it can't buy a home.

Money can buy influence, but it can't buy friendship. Money can buy sex, but it can't buy love. Money can buy just about anything, except happiness and joy. Money can take you just about anywhere except to God. Jesus says, "**Come to me**," when you have tried everything else and you have run out of options and when you have no other place to run."

You might be asking why should I listen? Can I help you and tell you about the one who is inviting you to come is the one who:

…revives hearts.

…refreshes souls.

…renews love.

…replenishes joy.

…restores confidence.

…relieves pressures.

…regenerate life.

Jesus reminds you and I that when we are weary, worn and worried He is the One that can give rest where we need it the most - not in your body, but in your soul.

Jesus not only invites us to *"come to Him"* in prayer when we are weary, worn and worried. He invites us to "take His yoke" in prayer.

After you come to Jesus there is something you must take from Jesus *²⁹ **Take my yoke upon you...*** That doesn't really sound too inviting, does it? A yoke, as you know, is a wooden bar made to fit around the neck and the shoulders of an ox. The farmer would attach a harness to the yoke and then the farmer could control the ox and guide it anywhere he wanted it to go. The yoke is a symbol of submission. It is a symbol of surrender.

There are two problems with this picture that comes naturally to mind. First, nobody wants to be under anyone's yoke. We want to be totally free and do what we want to do, go where we want to go, and be who we want to be. The second problem is we do not want to be pulling a burden, especially a heavy one. We have enough problems of our own without pulling somebody else's weight, worry or weakness. Before you reject the yoke, Jesus is offering and the burden, He is asking you to carry, listen to what He says about both. ³⁰ **For my yoke is easy, and my burden is light."**

Jesus said, "***my yoke is easy.***" The word ***easy*** means, *"excellent, good, and perfectly suited for its purpose."* Frequently, a good farmer would hire a carpenter to custom carve a yoke to fit the chosen ox to the point the ox would not even know it was around his neck. This enabled the ox or donkey to pull a plow for many hours without blistering or chaffing.

This is why Jesus went on to say, "**my burden is light.**" Here is what Jesus is telling us. Do you want to be free? Freedom is not being out of control and is not being under no one's control. Freedom is being under the right control.

In war, peace will never come until one side surrenders to the other. I would even suggest this great country that you and I are privileged to live in, will never live up to her name, the United States of America, until we are able to set aside our political parties, policies and self-promotions and surrender. The same thing is true in life. Every day is a battle and you will not have rest or peace until you surrender your life to Jesus. Let me put it to you this way. The only way to get free from the concerns of life is to surrender to the control of Christ.

Allow me to be transparent for a moment. Please do not judge me because all of God's children have issues. My issue I want to share with you is I have a problem surrendering my life. Now you might think it strange, but please hear me out. I, like many of you, have given my life to Jesus Christ through the plan of salvation. First, I confessed that I was in desperate need of a Savior and God was not first place in my life. Secondly, I believed Jesus became the perfect sin offering for me through His death, burial, and His resurrection on the third day. Thirdly, I confessed Jesus Christ the Son of God as my Lord and Savior and invited Him into my life. And lastly, I gave my life to becoming a doer of His word rather than just a hearer. My confession, however, is I am still struggling and straining with surrendering, giving up my will for His will.

One day William Booth the founder of the Salvation Army was asked what was his secret to the peace in his life? They asked, "How is it that you can rest when no one else can?" Mr. Booth replied, "Because I never say, No to the Lord." This was a man who had found the right Master. This was a man who had put on the yoke of Jesus and he found that yoke easy and that burden to be light. That's my goal in life. I want to reach the point where I never say no to the Lord. How about you? I want to trust Him better. I want to surrender more of my life today than I did on yesterday. He desires it. He deserves it. He demands it. And He delights in it.

Jesus is not a taskmaster. He is a tender master. He is not a hard shepherd that beats, bruises, or talks bad to His sheep. He is a loving shepherd that leads His sheep. The only places the Good Shepherd will ever lead you and I are the places best for us. He leads us to the places we can rest in Him.

Our shepherd will only lead us to places where:

He can watch over us.

He can protect us.

He can keep us.

He can supply us.

He can comfort us.

He can lift us.

Our shepherd will only lead us to the places where we can find rest:

Regardless of our troubles, trails and tests.

Regardless of our circumstances.

Regardless of our dilemmas, dangers and difficulties.

Regardless of our sin, sorrow and sadness.

Regardless of our hardship, heartaches and headaches.

Regardless of our miseries, mess ups and mishaps.

There is nothing that will cause you more stress than to refuse or throw off the yoke of Jesus. When you live for Jesus you will have a conscience that is clear and a soul at rest.

Jesus invites us to **"learn from me***"* in prayer when we find ourselves weary, worn and worried.

When you come to Jesus you begin school where He is the teacher, and the main subject. Why?

Nobody faced more stress than Jesus.

Nobody was under more pressure than Jesus.

Nobody carried a heavier burden than Jesus.

Nobody dealt with as much hatred than Jesus.

Nobody came in contact with as much disease than Jesus.

So, He advises us, "Watch how I handle the tough times. Look at how I handled the difficult people. Watch how I managed the troubling circumstances." From the day He was born to a virgin named Mary, wrapped in swaddling clothes in a manager there was a hit put out on Him from King Herod. From the day Jesus Christ began His ministry He went to people who were standing in line crying out, "Touch me, bless me, heal me, help me, hear me, and teach me. He never lost His peace on the inside and never lost His patience on the outside. From the moment He lifted the cross on His shoulder, it was a reminder of how He carried the weight of the entire world's sin, sorrow, and suffering.

Someone wisely shared, "There is absolutely nothing you can earn from Jesus, but there is a tremendous amount you can learn from Jesus." Some days it is stormy. We all get weary in the fight. We all get to a point when we can't take another step. This is why Jesus wants us to sit at His feet every day and not just learn about Him but learn from Him also. What Jesus teaches you will revolutionize your life. You will find the way He speaks to you is relaxing and you will find when He walks with you it is refreshing.

Let me tell you something about being a Christian and a follower of Jesus. I have had people reject accepting Jesus Christ as their Lord and Savior. Why, you ask? Because they believed it is too hard to be a Christian. Can I tell you what I learned? I have learned it is much harder to be a sinner than a saint any day. You see, sinners have to pay for every sin done in their body. As a saint we have already been given the victory through Christ Jesus who died for us. When you are a slave to the world, the enemy is a harsh, hard and horrible taskmaster. However, when you come to Jesus, you will find His yoke is not easy. Are you getting the point? Let me tell you what I have seen with my own eyes. Compared to sexual, drug, alcohol or money addiction, life is so much easier when you are looking for, living for, and learning from Jesus. Matthew is the only one of the four gospel writers, to have recorded this invitation from Jesus. I believe it is because he was once a tax collector. He once thought the way to handle stress is to get all you can, get to the top, and call your own shots until He met Jesus. Do you desire to live a life free from worry, stress, and wanting more? The only way to this life is to give up everything you want and accept what Jesus wants to give you. When Jesus is all you have, He is everything you need.

3 A PRAYER OF FAITH IN THE MIDST OF FEAR AND FAILURE

---

²²Immediately he made the disciples get into the boat and go before him to the other side, while he dismissed the crowds. ²³And after he had dismissed the crowds, he went up on the mountain by himself to pray. When evening came, he was there alone, ²⁴but the boat by this time was a long way from the land, beaten by the waves, for the wind was against them. ²⁵And in the fourth watch of the night he came to them, walking on the sea. ²⁶But when the disciples saw him walking on the sea, they were terrified, and said, "It is a ghost!" and they cried out in fear. ²⁷But immediately Jesus spoke to them, saying, "Take heart; it is I. Do not be afraid." ²⁸And Peter answered him, "Lord, if it is you, command me to come to you on the water." ²⁹He said, "Come." So, Peter got out of the boat and walked on the water and came to Jesus. ³⁰But when he saw the wind, he was afraid, and beginning to sink he cried out, "Lord, save me." ³¹Jesus immediately reached out his hand and took hold of him, saying to him, "O you of little faith, why did you doubt?" ³²And when they got into the boat, the wind ceased. ³³And those in the boat worshiped him, saying, "Truly you are the Son of God." Matthew 14:22-33

"All of us are born with this set of instinctive fears. The fear of falling. The fear of the dark. The fear of speaking in front of a group of people. The fear of failure, of loss, of rejection, and there is even the fear of the future. ~ Author Unknown

Here is today's statement of fact. We all have fears. Here is an additional statement of fact. God is not surprised by our fears. Several times in the Holy Bible, God instructs His children to "Fear not!" This statement is found over 366 times in the Bible. Someone wisely said there is a "fear not," for every day of the year plus leap year! One might have thought God would have commanded us to "Love one another" 366 times; but instead, He instructed us to "Fear not!"

God does not want us to allow fear to cripple, crush or consume us. **Joshua 1:9 says, Have I not commanded you? Be strong and courageous. Do not be frightened, and do not be dismayed, for the LORD your God is with you wherever you go."**

I know you're thinking and saying, "Pastor I hear you, but after this past year with a pandemic, politics, panic, protesting, police brutality and pandemonium around the world, I have to admit I am fearful.

So, let us talk about fear for a moment.

the fears that keep us from living life to its fullest.

the fears that keep us from being fully alive.

the fears that keep us from being the person God created us to be.

Take a moment and imagine you are able to start your life over. You are old enough to know right from wrong. You have learned a few lessons, experienced real love and are old enough to really live. With that in mind, if you could ask the Lord Jesus Christ to make the rest of your life the best days of your life, what do you think He would say? In my sanctified imagination I believe He would tell us, "Do not be afraid of failure."

Failure is not the reality of an event, but rather it is the response to an event. Failure does not shape a person. It is the response to failure that shapes a person. I remember hearing Dr. Adrian Rogers say, "Failure need not be fatal and it does not have to be final."

As a young pastor I would share the story of Peter walking on water when I talked about failure. After all, once he began to walk on water he started to sink. Now that I am a more experienced and knowledgeable Pastor, I realize this story is one of the greatest stories of success in the Bible. It marks, not only a life that took a risk, but a life completely obedient to the will of God.

There are two categories of people in the story. There are those who because of fear did nothing. And then there is Peter who, because of faith did something. Let me paint the picture for you. This storm was much more than an afternoon shower. The Scripture tells us of a violent storm where the winds and waves were beating against the boat. Verses 22-23 say, **²² Immediately he made the disciples get into the boat and go before him to the other side, while he dismissed the crowds. ²³ And after he had dismissed the crowds, he went up on the mountain by himself to pray. When evening came, he was there alone…"**

Isn't it interesting Jesus put his disciples on a ship He knew was going to run directly into a storm? The phrase "he made" literally means, Jesus compelled or begged His disciples to go to the other side. In other words, Jesus begged His disciples to get into the boat. And He did so with full knowledge of the storm brewing.

Why would Jesus send His disciples into a storm? This storm took place right after a major miracle in the life of Jesus. Jesus had just taken 5 loaves and 2 fish and fed at least 5000 men, not counting women and children.

This reminds us there will be times when God allows us to enjoy a great victory right on the heels of a grievous vice. We may be on the mountaintop now, but before long we have to come back down into the valley.

This is the point when I have a few questions. My first question is why would Jesus send them into such a severe storm? Should it not have been a milder storm to test their faith? Surely Jesus would not send His disciples directly into an awful and angry storm? The Scripture answers to the contrary.

We read in verse 24, "**but the boat by this time was a long way from the land, beaten by the waves, for the wind was against them.**" The word 'beaten' literally means 'to torment, or strain.' In other words, the vehement winds were beating so violently against the ship that the disciples were having trouble keeping the ship on course. This ship was bobbing up and down on the raging waves like a loose piece of garbage. It was a storm of great intensity.

Here is the point I believe this text is tailored to teach us. There is no pass that we are given that excludes us from "the storms of life." The Bible never promises a life free from suffering, sickness, sorrow or storms. In fact, many times the Lord Jesus in His Sovereign wisdom sends us directly into the midst of a storm.

We must remember, God's intention is never to break us down. It is to build us up. His desire is not to make us bitter but better. He wants not to hurt us but help us. Storms are not intended to drive us from God, but to God. Rest assured, behind every storm we can find that God's weather forecast is to push us into what He has purposed and planned for our lives.

In this story we discover the anxiety and fear of the disciples. And before we get too spiritual, I believe it is safe to say if we were in the disciples' shoes, we would have been frightened as well.

Let's walk through the rest of the story [in my best Paul Harvey voice]. There were 12 disciples on the ship. All were filled with fear, anxiety and cowardice. We read in verses 25-27, **²⁵And in the fourth watch of the night he came to them, walking on the sea. ²⁶But when the disciples saw him walking on the sea, they were terrified, and said, "It is a ghost!" and they cried out in fear. ²⁷But immediately Jesus spoke to them, saying, "Take heart; it is I. Do not be afraid."**

Picture it. The water is calm. The sun is bright and the air is still. Imagine Peter, James, John and the rest of the crew laid diamond in the back, sunroof top, digging the scene with a disciple lean, wooh-wooh. Then, suddenly, the waves are crashing in and the wind is forceful. It is three o'clock in the morning, and they thought they saw a ghost.

The word 'ghost' in verse 26 is the Greek word 'phantasma'. It speaks of a shiny, invisible image that suddenly becomes visible. When they saw Jesus, they did not recognize Him. Their first inclination, given the current weather conditions, was that He was a ghost. The storm had distorted their vision of the Lord Jesus. They are scared to death.

And they cried out in fear. (v.26) The word "fear" comes from an Old English word for danger. The disciples perplexing fear paralyzed them, cheating them out of a real blessing. There was, however, one man who conjured up enough courage not to stand cowardly by. Peter decided to face his fear head on. He decided to do something. Peter had the courage, in the midst of the worst storm he had ever faced, to get out of the boat and walk to Jesus. Unlike the other disciples he did not allow his fear to paralyze him.

How do we know? In verse 27, Jesus says to the disciples, **"Take heart; it is I. Do not be afraid."** In verse 28, Peter makes the request, **"Lord, if it is you, command me to come to you on the water."** And finally, in verse 29, we read, **Jesus said, "Come." So, Peter got out of the boat and walked on the water and came to Jesus."**

Now, before you begin to criticize and crucify Peter because of what happens next. Pause and celebrate with me the fact Peter got out of the boat. Isn't it funny how the cowardice individuals who choose to stay in the boat, where things are comfortable and certain, are the ones to condemn the ones who stepped out on faith? What is faith except a courageous step out into the deep waters where things are uncomfortable and uncertain?

I can only imagine what the "boat crowd" must have been saying. Perhaps they said, "Peter, what in the world is wrong with you? Don't you know it is raining outside? Do you not have the commonsense God gave you to know you cannot walk on water?"

I want to pause right now and speak to the individual reading this who is contemplating stepping out on faith into unchartered territory. I want to warn you that whenever you decide to do something for God you will encounter "the boat crowd". You already know who they are. They are the ones who talk you out of finishing your degree, starting a business, trying something new, fresh and exciting because they have no desire themselves to ever get out of the boat. They have spent their entire lives hanging around you to pour water on your fire. They have no intention or interest in doing anything for God. They only take pleasure in criticizing those who are serving God.

I don't mean to spend so much time on the "boat crowd", but the Holy Spirit will not let me leave this place yet. In 29 years of ministry, I have experienced many individuals who are in that crowd. They are the ones who says, "We have never done it that way before. What if things don't work out like you think they should? It's too expensive. Someone else tried and it didn't work. No one is going to support that."

Can I testify for a minute? I hear the "boat crowd" every week. They say things like "He preached too long. He fusses too much. The music is too loud. The choir sang too long. Here he goes asking us to by another book. He is not going to get rich off me. I would get involved, but I am just too busy. I will do it when things slowdown."

Serving God is not meant to be convenient! There will always be something that hinders us from serving God if we let it. The church is full of Christians who blow hot air and never show. They talk a good game, but do not walk it out. They have stipulations to their service. It really isn't about God; it is about them.

I have been told there are three classes of people: those who make things happen, those who watch things happen, and those who do not know what happened. The "boat crowd" watches what happens, and the water-walkers make things happen. If you are going to do something for God, then you must get out of the boat. The time has come for you to stop talking, and instead, start walking. Fear has ended and your faith walk has begun.

Here it is straight no chaser. You will never walk on the water and do anything for God until you muster up enough courage to handle the criticism of the "boat crowd" and get out of the boat. Let the "boat crowd" talk, because that is all they will ever do. The only time you will not have to deal with the "boat crowd" is if you stay safely tucked away in the expectations and limitations they place on you. Believe me when I tell you, when you decide to totally surrender and serve God, you will hear criticism. Go ahead and get out of the boat anyway! Even if you begin to sink, you will find Jesus ready, willing and able to help you. I like how the late great Walter Hawkins says it in his song, God Is Standing By.

"Everywhere you go there is trouble (there is trouble)

Everywhere you go there is strife (there is strife)

Everywhere you go there is something that worries you

But remember (my God is standing by),

No need to cry (God is standing near),

No need to fear. Jesus, He'll be right there, (He's everywhere)

Yes (He'll hear you when you pray)

oh yes (He'll catch you before you fall)

oh yes (He'll guide you until the end)

My God is standing by"

Let's get back to the story so you can shout with me. Jesus appears, walking on the water, in the midst of a horrific storm. Peter's faith rises up within him as he says in verse 28, ***"Lord, if it is you, command me to come..."*** Jesus responds with one word in verse 29, ***"Come!"*** That was all the assurance Peter needed. Once he is certain of Jesus' presence, he steps out of the boat and begins to walk toward Him.

Notice Peter was looking for direction from the Lord not a promise he would not fail. He didn't say, "Lord, if it is You, promise me that I won't sink." He said, **"Lord, if it is you, command me to come to you." (v.28)** Peter was grateful for the opportunity to walk.

If God has called you to do something, what are you waiting for? Get out of the boat!

If God has placed a burden in your heart for a specific ministry, get out of the boat!

If God has whispered to you in His still, small voice, then forget about everything else and get out of the boat!

I cannot stress enough how important this concept is to every child of God. Contrary to the opinion of the majority, upon the command of Jesus, Peter gets out of the boat. So, where did Peter go wrong? Why did his faith waiver? Because Peter gave into his doubts, fears and concerns. He took his eyes off Jesus, saw the severity of the storm, and began to sink. When he realized Jesus was still there, he prays one of the greatest prayers in the Bible, **"Lord, save me." (v.30)**

And without hesitation, **[31] Jesus immediately reached out his hand and took hold of him, saying to him, "O you of little faith, why did you doubt?" [32] And when they got into the boat, the wind ceased. (vv.31-32)** Did you picture what happened in the moment Peter asked Jesus to save him? Jesus responded immediately. It stands to reason if Peter had not gotten out of the boat, God would never have had the opportunity to manifest His glory and power in the storm.

I want you to think about something. I need you to erase everything you have ever heard about the failure of Peter. Peter did begin to fall, but he did not fail. The failures of the story were the eleven disciples who stayed in the boat.

If you are not interested in living out your God-given purpose, then stay right in your comfort zone. However, if you are one of the individuals who have crucified self and desire to bring glory and honor to God, you must take the first step. Why? Because that is where Jesus is. He's not in the boat of comfort, but He is walking on the very thing that would otherwise hinder you.

Wouldn't it be a tragedy to know God has given us everything we need to do something great for Him, and yet we never do it? The choice is yours. You can stay in the boat, and do nothing, or you can get out of the boat and do something. You cannot have both.

4 A PRAYER OF TRIUMPH IN TIMES OF TESTING

[36] Then Jesus went with them to a place called Gethsemane, and he said to his disciples, "Sit here, while I go over there and pray." [37] And taking with him Peter and the two sons of Zebedee, he began to be sorrowful and troubled. [38] Then he said to them, "My soul is very sorrowful, even to death; remain here, and watch with me." [39] And going a little farther he fell on his face and prayed, saying, "My Father, if it be possible, let this cup pass from me; nevertheless, not as I will, but as you will."

Matthew 26:36-39

I want to begin this chapter with a question. What is your prayer routine? Is it your practice to petition God with a laundry list of requests? Do your prayers sound like a selfish toddler saying time after time? "Lord, this is what I want?" If this is you, you have missed out on the most important part of communing with God…listening.

Read the next two sentences out loud.

Prayer is not a method of manipulation; it is a means of cooperation. It is not me telling God what I want, but rather God telling me what He wants.

Evangelist Billy Graham said, "Prayer is spiritual communication between man and God, a two-way relationship in which man should not only talk to God but also listen to Him."

Prayer to God is like a child's conversation with his father. It is natural for a child to ask his father for the things he wants and needs. However, I believe Scripture also teaches us as we mature in Christ our prayers should be us talking less and listening more to the Father.

Prayer that is powerful and purposeful is when we raise from the posture of prayer with clear instruction and a premeditated yes. Prayer becomes powerful when we stop trying to bend God's will to our will and instead accept God's will. It is only when God's heart's desire becomes our heart's desire that prayer is true and effectual.

Prayer is submission to hear, do, respond and act upon what God says.

As we make our transition into today's passage, I want to present an important concept you must have under your belt. This text opens up with our Lord and Savior Jesus Christ in prayer in the garden of Gethsemane shortly before His hour of destiny. It is here Jesus utters nine important words, ***"nevertheless, not as I will, but as you will."***

To understand what our Lord was being faced with here, we must remember the trials He had encountered along the way. Jesus had a productive, but not always a pleasant earthly ministry. The fact He was the second part of the Trinity did not exempt Him from facing ridicule, rejection, reproach and removal.

Jesus began teaching in the synagogue at the age of twelve with wit, wonder and wisdom. There were those skeptics who questioned his authority on the subjects He taught. He began to explain His purpose for coming to earth from the very beginning. He outlined the strain, struggle and stress He dealt with daily in **John 1:11. "He came unto his own, and his own people did not receive him!"**

Think of the times the Pharisees tried to set Him up. **Mark 12:13 says, "And they sent to him some of the Pharisees and some of the Herodians, to trap him in his talk."** It seemed as if their entire mission was to trap Him, test Him and try Him. **John 15:18** is also another reference point to what Jesus encountered. **"If the world hates you, know that it has hated me before it hated you."**

Shortly after His arrest there was the tragic denial by Peter, a man who was one of the inner circle of the disciples found in **Luke 22:54-62.** **⁵⁴Then they seized him and led him away, bringing him into the high priest's house, and Peter was following at a distance. ⁵⁵And when they had kindled a fire in the middle of the courtyard and sat down together, Peter sat down among them. ⁵⁶Then a servant girl, seeing him as he sat in the light and looking closely at him, said, "This man also was with him." ⁵⁷But he denied it, saying, "Woman, I do not know him." ⁵⁸And a little later someone else saw him and said, "You also are one of them." But Peter said, "Man, I am not." ⁵⁹And after an interval of about an hour still another insisted, saying, "Certainly this man also was with him, for he too is a Galilean." ⁶⁰But Peter said, "Man, I do not know what you are talking about." And immediately, while he was still speaking, the rooster crowed. ⁶¹And the Lord turned and looked at Peter. And Peter remembered the saying of the Lord, how he had said to him, "Before the rooster crows today, you will deny me three times." ⁶²And he went out and wept bitterly.**

Through it all the Jews denounced Him, the scribes doubted Him, the traitor defrauded Him, the soldiers despised Him, and one of His closest servants denied Him. The icing on the cake is found in **Matthew 26:45. Then he came to the disciples and said to them,**

"Sleep and take your rest later on. See, the hour is at hand, and the Son of Man is betrayed into the hands of sinners." Do you get it? At the completion of His prayer in Gethsemane, He comes to His disciples and His inner circle was sleep.

Jesus' life was full of twists and turns, but in spite of the journey that was behind Him there was a job before Him He was determined to complete. The moment of destiny had arrived. The task for which He came to earth was now upon Him. There was no avoiding it. There was no eluding it. There was no abstaining from it. The time had come, and the cross and crucifixion was before Jesus.

Jesus' arrest was not the end of His ministry, but the beginning. It was not the completion of His ministry, but the culmination. It was not the period, but the exclamation point. Listen, I must stop here and encourage you as you read these words. Never allow anyone to step into your life and put a period where God has put a comma. And certainly, never allow anyone to put a period where God has put an exclamation point.

Let's read verse 37. **And taking with him Peter and the two sons of Zebedee, he began to be sorrowful and troubled.** Jesus is expressing the anguish, agony and aching of the physical and spiritual pain He was facing. Remember, Jesus was both God and man. I don't know about you, but this encourages me. In my time of sorrow and trouble, it is good to know He knows. Proof of this is found in **Luke**

22:44. "And being in an agony he prayed more earnestly; and his sweat became like great drops of blood falling down to the ground."

Notice how He describes it to His disciples in verse 38. **Then he said to them, "My soul is very sorrowful, even to death; remain here, and watch with me."** The phrase 'very sorrowful' speaks of "being overwhelmed, or extremely troubled." This is the same word used by our Lord in **John 12:27**, when he said to His disciples, **"Now is my soul troubled. And what shall I say? 'Father, save me from this hour'? But for this purpose, I have come to this hour."** This was the moment of truth for the world for which He came.

As William Barclay in his commentary of The Gospel of Matthew, Vol. 2, said, "The salvation of the world was at risk in Gethsemane. This was no play-acting; but it was a struggle in which the outcome swayed in the balance." Jesus' travail was so great He makes the most urgent request ever made, [39] **"My Father, if it be possible, let this cup pass from me."**

Theologians have debated for centuries what Jesus saw in that cup. Many have concluded what He saw almost made Him retreat. I personally believe when He looked into that cup, He saw you and me. He saw our depravity, despondency and defilement.

Jesus saw our sins and His suffering.

He saw the just suffering for the unjust.

He saw the holy suffering for the unholy.

He saw the best suffering for the worst.

There was not one thought of retreat in our Savior's mind. This was the final piece to the puzzle of His earthly ministry. He endured the anguish to prove every one of us will have a Gethsemane. We will all have a moment when we will feel the weight of completing our assignment here on earth. We will need to pray for strength. We will need to be reminded that our Father's will is what is most important.

Some of you reading this may be experiencing a Gethsemane moment. You may find yourself wrestling with the forces of darkness and hell. You are not alone. There have been times in my own life when I have been in such a spiritual struggle. I thought I was losing my mind. It felt as if the walls of everything I have preached, believed in and held on to were collapsing around me.

Do you find yourself at the point of exhaustion?

Do you find yourself in something today that has you saying, **"Father, if it be possible, let this cup pass from me?"** Our Lord did.

As we come to the end of our time today, there is an amazing and incredible shift in the prayer Jesus prayed. We sense the heaviness and excruciating pressure and pain rise to the highest point as our Lord and Savior Jesus Christ shouts, "Nevertheless!"

Look with me at verse 39. **And going a little farther he fell on his face and prayed, saying, "My Father, if it be possible, let this cup pass from me; <u>nevertheless</u>, not as I will, but as you will."** Here is the turning point for Jesus. It did not matter what Jesus had encountered to this point in His ministry. Everything swings on this one verse. And I do not know about you, but I am thankful that with all of the hardship, heartache and heartbreak Jesus endured, He still had a hunger to do the will of God.

You might lose your house. You might even want to quit. I encourage you today never lose your hunger to know and do the will of God. There is no doubt in my mind there are some who are reading this, who have not faithfully studied the Bible, prayed passionately, worshiped the wonder of the Lord or served God and His people. How many times have we settled with a 'microwaveable approach' to prayer in order to know the will of God?

I need to pause and place a footnote here and say, it does you no good to have a hunger to know the will of God and not a heart to do the will of God. Notice verse 39. **And going a little farther he fell on his face and prayed, saying, "My Father, if it be possible, let this cup pass from me; nevertheless, not as I will, but as you will."**

While He had a hunger to know the will of God, He also had a heart to do the will of God.

You see ladies and gentlemen, it was His hunger that brought Him to the garden; but it was His heart that carried Him through the garden. When He approached His Sovereign Father there was no thought of manipulating His will, only mastering His will. He was not confused about His Father's will, only cooperating with His will. As we close today's devotional reading let me ask you a question. Do you have a hunger to know the will of God for your life? If so, do you have a heart to do the will of God in your life with no hesitation? Then like our blessed Redeemer, in spite of the trial, you will experience triumph for the journey!

The Blueprints

An engineer was confined to his bed, his lower limbs being paralyzed, but because of his reputation for great skill he was asked to draw the blueprints for a great suspension bridge. The plans were completed and placed in the hands of those who were to do the work. Months passed by and the bridge was finished. Four men came to the engineer's room and carried him out on his cot to a place from whence he could view the bridge spanning a wide river, over which vehicles were rapidly passing. Tears filled his eyes, and looking down at the blueprints in his hands, he cried out, "It's just like the plan; it's just like the plan." God has His blueprints. They are world plans; others are individual life plans. Have we found His plan for our lives, and are we obediently walking therein? There can be no greater reward when looking back over our lives from eternity, than to hear Him say, "It's just like the plan; it's just like the plan."—*The Wonderful Word.*

I will leave you today with one thought. Is your desire to do the will of God without hesitation and with anticipation? And once you find out His will for your life are you willing to follow it?

5 A PRAYER OF PERSISTENCE IN A HOPELESS SITUATION

¹And he told them a parable to the effect that they ought always to pray and not lose heart. ² He said, "In a certain city there was a judge who neither feared God nor respected man. ³ And there was a widow in that city who kept coming to him and saying, 'Give me justice against my adversary. ⁴ For a while he refused, but afterward he said to himself, 'Though I neither fear God nor respect man, ⁵ yet because this widow keeps bothering me, I will give her justice, so that she will not beat me down by her continual coming.'" ⁶ And the Lord said, "Hear what the unrighteous judge says. ⁷And will not God give justice to his elect, who cry to him day and night? Will he delay long over them? ⁸I tell you, he will give justice to them speedily. Nevertheless, when the Son of Man comes, will he find faith on earth?" Luke 18:1-8

Jesus says we "**ought always to pray**". This is the idea we find in **1 Thessalonians 5:17**, where the Bible says, "**Pray without ceasing.**" "*Without ceasing*" means "*no intermission*". Jesus is telling us to "*ready ourselves, be on guard, and be watchful.*" It is the idea of being in the attitude and atmosphere of prayer all the time. You see, prayer is more than an obligation. It is also an opportunity. An opportunity for us to be in touch with our heavenly Father any time the need arises!

Not only are we to always pray, Jesus says we are not to give up. This phrase means "*to not faint, to not give up, never quit, never become discouraged, never become slothful, to not grow weary*". Jesus challenges His people not to lose heart during the times when the answer to prayer is delayed. Don't give up, keep praying! God will move in His time! This is precisely why Paul writes in **Galatians 6:9, "And let us not grow weary of doing good, for in due season we will reap, if we do not give up!"**

There is a story about a well-known NCAA football coach who sent one of his assistants on a recruiting trip. They were in search for a certain type of athlete to fill some holes in the team game plan. When the assistant coach reached his destination, he immediately made his way to the practice field to get a look at the team. He watched for a little while and then with great excitement he picks up his cellphone to call the head coach. "Coach, I have found just what we are looking for." He began to describe the player to the coach. "This player,

although knocked down, would get back up every time. We need him."
Much to the assistant coach's surprise, the head coach disagreed. He
responded by saying, "It is not the one who continues to get back up,
I need the one who does the knocking down." The principle is how
we should look at the power of persistent prayer. We must be
persistent enough to keep on knocking, asking, and seeking no matter
what.

Sadly, too many people do not practice this in their prayer life.
They pray about something for a while and when the answer does not
come when they think it should, they just throw up their hands in
defeat and say, "What's the use?" How many times have you given up
too soon? You may not admit it to anyone; however, I have a sneaky
suspicion at some point in your walk with God you felt like praying
was useless. And it is this type of thinking the enemy loves. He knows
there is power in prayer and if he can plant the seed of doubt, he feels
he has won.

Today's verse, the Lord Jesus tells His disciples a parable
designed to teach them the importance of remaining persistent in
prayer. This principle is extremely important, so much so that the one
who really gets it will experience a changed life. Everything in our lives
depends on prayer! My childhood Pastor, Dr. John A. Reed, Jr. taught
us, "that it happens after prayer." I am not sure what you need God to
do in your life spiritually, emotionally, financially, relationally,

intellectually, physically or occupationally. I will tell you nothing will change in those areas without persistent, unrelenting prayer. You must have a burden for prayer.

One of the very first things we see is the widow's pain. Verse 3 reads, **And there was a widow in that city who kept coming to him and saying, 'Give me justice against my adversary.'** We are not told the nature of this woman's burden, only that she had a grievance against someone lying very heavily upon her heart. Notice, this poor widow woman had several things working against her. The first thing is her sex. She was a woman and women were not allowed to speak in court. Secondly, she was a widow. There was no husband to speak on her behalf. And lastly, it was a foregone conclusion, widows were a part of society that was oppressed and often taken advantage of. And yet, with all those things working against her, she did not stop pleading her case.

In verse 5, we see the persistence of the woman pay off. **"... yet because this widow keeps bothering me...."** She showed up at court every day begging the judge to do something about her grievance. When he would show up for court, there she was. When he went into the marketplace, there she was. When he was out on the golf course, she kept bothering him. She pleaded with him in the company of his neighbors. She stalked him at home while he was having dinner with his family. She kept bothering him. Everywhere he went, there she was, constantly asking him to give her satisfaction.

This poor, widow woman made a nuisance of herself before the judge, every day, until she received the very thing she was after! Can I stop here just long enough to tell you, this widow represents you and me. Let's be honest here. There are times when we are burdened down with cares, worries, fears and troubles. During those times, it may seem the circumstances of life is stacked against us. We may be tempted to ask God:

"Why don't you answer my prayer?"

"What are you up to?"

"Why don't you do something?"

"When are you going to do something?"

"Where are you right now?"

If this is you or has been you, this widow woman's story is for you. God wanted you to know persistence and perseverance in prayer will pay off. We must learn to wait on God's timing! So, keep praying, despite all the obstacles you face and the signs you see telling you to give up.

There is another point I want to show you. Jesus says, **"In a certain city there was a judge who neither feared God nor respected man. (v.2)** The widow knew she was presenting her case to someone who did not believe in God. Times may be tough in your world right now. It may appear the ones in charge neither fear God nor respect man. I want to encourage you not to let that stop you from praying. God is able to even use the wicked to bless His children. Warren Weirsbe in his commentary "Be Courageous," explains it this way. "The courtroom was not a fine building but a tent that was moved from place to place as the judge covered his circuit. The judge, not the law, set the agenda; and he sat regally in the tent, surrounded by his assistants. Anybody could watch the proceeding from outside, but only those who were approved and accepted could have their cases tried. This usually meant bribing one of the assistants so that he could call the judges attention to the case. This is still true in much of the third world countries today."

Even though he had heard this widow's petition, he would not rule in her favor. Day after day he turned a deaf ear to her pleas for help. Now that was cold blooded (I just dated myself). This judge was callous and after a period of time became condescending. I hear you, Pastor G, but punching sounds a lot better than praying at this point. Thank God his spiritual condition did not stop God from working. In verse 5 we find these words. **"Yet because this widow keeps bothering me, I will give her justice, so that she will not beat me down by her continual coming."** There are two phrases in this verse of special interest. The first one is **"keeps bothering me"**. The word bothering comes from two words that mean, "*to reach forth to beat another or to cause another trouble.*" The second is **"beat me down"** which means "*to wear down, to blacken the eye*". It is a phrase used to describe the effects of being beaten severely about the head. Evidently the widow's persistence was hurting his reputation and giving him a "*black eye*" in the community!

Here is the point. Please do not miss it. There may be times when we pray and may not get the answer we want immediately, but we must keep praying. We cannot forget God is God and we are not. God will answer in His time! Quit whining and whimpering and put your focus back where it belongs, on God. There is nothing more important than keeping your focus on God's plan, purpose, and priorities.

In the middle of tough times and dark days, renew your remembrance of who God is and what He has done. Remind yourself the sovereign God can be trusted. This knowledge will help you avoid some sleepless nights and lonesome days. You ready? God is eternal and His ways are eternal. The circumstances around you change, but God doesn't. The same God who created the universe is the same God who looks after you. Things change on earth every day, but they never change in eternity. God's principles, promises, and purpose never change. He may change His methods and may change His timing, but

His ability never changes. No matter the circumstance, He is still an omnipresent, omniscient, and omnipotent God.

George Mueller said, "The great fault of the children of God is, they do not continue in prayer; they do not go on praying; they do not persevere!"

Now here's something to encourage you to throw the book down and call me some bad names. Watch Jesus turn from the character in this parable to the Father up in Heaven. He shows us that God, who is nothing like the unjust judge, delights in answering the prayers of His people. We need never to fear that God doesn't hear us, because His ear is forever open to the cry of His children, **[7]And will not God give justice to his elect, who cry to him day and night?"**

Before they call I will answer; while they are yet speaking I will hear. Isaiah 65:24

Call to me and I will answer you, and will tell you great and hidden things that you have not known. Jeremiah 33:3

**[14]And this is the confidence that we have toward him, that if we ask anything according to his will he hears us. [15]And if we know that he hears us in whatever we ask, we know that we have the requests that we have asked of him.
1 John 5:14-15**

Verse 7 goes on to say, **"Will he delay long over them?"** There will be times our prayers are answered immediately. Other times, the answer is delayed. The key is not giving up! God is not making us wait just because He can. He is working out the answers we seek. Our persistence in prayer demonstrates the depth of our burden. If you can pray about something once or twice and then give up, you were not really burdened over it. A genuine burden will put you before God and keep you there until He answers!

In truth, real prayer is the evidence of God's impending answer. How? Because real prayer always begins with God. The Spirit burdens our hearts and we offer the burden back to God, who is already engaged in bringing about the answer. **Romans 8:26-27** tells us, [26] **Likewise the Spirit helps us in our weakness. For we do not know what to pray for as we ought, but the Spirit himself intercedes for us with groanings too deep for words.** [27] **And he who searches hearts knows what is the mind of the Spirit, because the Spirit intercedes for the saints according to the will of God.** What great confidence that ought to give us in prayer! What a desire that should put within us to seek His face more consistently and persistently in prayer!

In verse 8 we find the final principle I want to share. **I tell you, he will give justice to them speedily. Nevertheless, when the Son of Man comes, will he find faith on earth?"** This verse may seem out of place, but it is not. Here it is in laymen's terms. "Will He find His people persisting in prayer before the Father over the things that really matter?" The answer to that question depends upon you and me!

Will He find a people of prayer? Will He find us persisting in prayer to the point our children and children's children are the benefactors of the answer? Verse 8 assures us even when we don't do what we are supposed to do, the Lord will keep every promise He ever made. He will be faithful to honor His Word to us. You may feel like giving up, but you keep on praying and He will answer in His time!

Pray on saints. The answer is on the way!

6 PRAYER TO BE IN HIS PRESENCE

---

*[9] He also told this parable to some who trusted in themselves that they were righteous, and treated others with contempt: [10] "Two men went up into the temple to pray, one a Pharisee and the other a tax collector. [11] The Pharisee, standing by himself, prayed thus: 'God, I thank you that I am not like other men, extortioners, unjust, adulterers, or even like this tax collector. [12] I fast twice a week; I give tithes of all that I get.' [13] But the tax collector, standing far off, would not even lift up his eyes to heaven, but beat his breast, saying, 'God, be merciful to me, a sinner!' [14] I tell you, this man went down to his house justified, rather than the other. For everyone who exalts himself will be humbled, but the one who humbles himself will be exalted." [15] Now they were bringing even infants to him that he might touch them. And when the disciples saw it, they rebuked them. [16] But Jesus called them to him, saying, "Let the children come to me, and do not hinder them, for to such belongs the kingdom of God. [17] Truly, I say to you, whoever does not receive the kingdom of God like a child shall not enter it." **Luke 18:9-17**

There will be years in our lives that serve as pivots. These years will be remembered in our life story as the moment when everything changes. 2020 has served as one of those years. It is the moment when I felt God was saying, "Choose ye this day whom you will serve." He was asking us to choose a side, not the Democrat or Republican side or the Black Lives or Blue Lives side. He wanted to see if in the middle of a pandemic, economic crisis and social unrest, if you will you represent me?

2020 will be remembered for the political circus that entertained us. The president of the United States faced two articles of impeachment and was later acquitted by the Senate. NBA legend Kobe Bryant was killed in a helicopter crash in Calabasas, California, along with his 13-year-old daughter Gianna and seven others, on Jan. 26th. On the same day of Kobe Bryant's funeral service in Los Angeles, Harvey Weinstein was convicted of rape and sexual assault in New York. February 4th the President delivered his State of the Union address and showed a public sign of disrespect by not shaking House Speaker Majority Leader, Nancy Pelosi's hand. She responded by ripping up his speech. And after that a pandemic entered the world. And as of December 2020, there have been over 17 million cases right here in the United States and over 300,00 deaths. The world shut down and as if things could not get any worse, the world witnessed the horrible death of George Floyd. For eight minutes and forty-six seconds, Derek Chauvine held his knee on Mr. Floyd's neck as he screamed for his mother in his last moments. This senseless act triggered protests around the world. 2020 was a pivotal year.

As hatred spread throughout the country, we experienced the most divisive election. For the first time in American history, our democracy was threatened with unsubstantiated voter fraud lawsuits. With all that said, one of the greatest challenges for me was the suspension of in-person worship. While many Christians took assembling together for granted, COVID-19 has made many appreciate fellowship with the body of Christ. The year 2020 will forever be remembered as the year the church was put on trial. Had we received enough of the Word of God to sustain us during this unprecedented time? March through May things seemed to be okay. June and July came and there was a major drop-off in online attendance. August through December, not many are left standing. It has been a very eye-opening experience. Those who had not already developed a lifestyle of private prayer, praise and reading God's Word have not fared well during this time.

2020 pushed the church to reimagine worship. We had to learn the importance of bringing God's House to our houses. I could have joined the majority complaining about where we were and even quit. I decided, instead, to look at this time as a great privilege. As you read this, I am not sure whether we will still be under physical gathering mandates or not. I am not sure if we will be worshiping virtual or in person. I do know, with confidence, prayer is essential in guaranteeing we worship God in spirit and in truth, the way He desires, demand and deserves.

I have a few questions for you today. How much preparation do you put into going to church? How much time do you spend getting your heart ready for corporate worship? Do you pray for the service? Do you seek the Lord's face and ask Him to move in power when we come together?" Do you pray for your Pastor? Do you saturate your mind, body and soul in the power of prayer for the purpose of meeting God the Father, God the Son and God the Holy Spirit?

I am afraid most of us, if we are honest, just come to church without giving what we are doing and why we are going a second thought. Did you know the Bible has something to say about how we are to go to church? Paul wrote in **1 Timothy 3:14-15** and said this. [14] **I hope to come to you soon, but I am writing these things to you so that, [15] if I delay, you may know how one ought to behave in the household of God, which is the church of the living God, a pillar and buttress of the truth.**

In **Ecclesiastes 5:1**, the preacher said, **Guard your steps when you go to the house of God. To draw near to listen is better than to offer the sacrifice of fools, for they do not know that they are doing evil.** In today's passage, the Lord Jesus allows us a glimpse into the Temple as people gathered to worship. We see one man came to church that day to worship himself and one came to church that day to worship the Lord. Let's examine these two individuals a little more closely. I believe there are some valuable lessons to be learned about how to come to church.

Warren Wiersbe in his Bible Exposition Commentary Be Courageous (Luke 14-24) writes, "Throughout His public ministry, Jesus exposed the self-righteousness and unbelief of the Pharisees (see **Luke 11:39-54**). He pictured them as debtors too bankrupt to pay what they owed God (**Luke 7:40-50**), guests fighting for the best seats (**Luke 14:7-14**), and sons proud of their obedience but unconcerned about the needs of others (**Luke 15:25-32**). The sad thing is the Pharisees were completely deluded and thought they were right, and Jesus was wrong."

I believe this concept is illustrated in this parable. We read in verse 9, **He also told this parable to some who trusted in themselves that they were righteous, and treated others with contempt**. He then introduced one of the men as a Pharisee. **"Two men went up into the temple to pray, one a Pharisee…"**

This Pharisee was a spiritual leader among the people. He was known and respected as a true man of God and knew Scriptures. Jesus said in **Matthew 23:5 They do all their deeds to be seen by others. For they make their phylacteries broad and their fringes long.**

This Pharisee had many passages committed to memory, and he even wore leather boxes on his right wrist and forehead that contained certain special portions of the Law. He would have prayed at least three times every day. Pharisees made much ado about prayer. They loved to pray loud, long and public prayers. **Matthew 6:5-6 [5] "And when you pray, you must not be like the hypocrites. For they love to stand and pray in the synagogues and at the street corners, that they may be seen by others. Truly, I say to you, they have received their reward. [6] But when you pray, go into your room and shut the door and pray to your Father who is in secret. And your Father who sees in secret will reward you.**

A Pharisee was required to fast twice every week. The Jews fasted on Mondays and Thursdays, which also happened to be the same days the Jews sold and bought wares in the markets. The practice of the Pharisees was to make their fasting very public. **Matthew 6:16-18** says, **[16] "And when you fast, do not look gloomy like the hypocrites, for they disfigure their faces that their fasting may be seen by others. Truly, I say to you, they have received their reward. [17] But when you fast, anoint your head and wash your face, [18] that your fasting may not be seen by others but by your Father who is in secret. And your Father who sees in secret will reward you.** They would not comb their hair or wash their faces. They wore the most wrinkled and rumpled clothes they could find. They even put ashes on their faces to make themselves look as though they were pale from fasting.

A Pharisee was required to tithe on everything he possessed, even the herbs grown in his garden. **Matthew 23:23 "Woe to you, scribes and Pharisees, hypocrites! For you tithe mint and dill and cumin and have neglected the weightier matters of the law: justice and mercy and faithfulness.** The Pharisees were noted for making a public show in their tithing. **Matthew 6:1-4** reads, [1] **"Beware of practicing your righteousness before other people in order to be seen by them, for then you will have no reward from your Father who is in heaven.** [2] **"Thus, when you give to the needy, sound no trumpet before you, as the hypocrites do in the synagogues and in the streets, that they may be praised by others. Truly, I say to you, they have received their reward.** [3] **But when you give to the needy, do not let your left hand know what your right hand is doing,** [4] **so that your giving may be in secret. And your Father who sees in secret will reward you.** Mark 12:41-44 says, [41] **And he sat down opposite the treasury and watched the people putting money into the offering box. Many rich people put in large sums.** [42] **And a poor widow came and put in two small copper coins, which make a penny.** [43] **And he called his disciples to him and said to them, "Truly, I say to you, this poor widow has put in more than all those who are contributing to the** offering box. **⁴⁴ For they all contributed out of their abundance, but she out of her poverty has put in everything she had, all she had to live on."**

A Pharisee was a very religious man, considered to be holy by everyone who saw him. He loved the adoration that came his way from the common people around him. **Matthew 23:5-7** says, **⁵ They do all their deeds to be seen by others. For they make their phylacteries broad and their fringes long, ⁶ and they love the place of honor at feasts and the best seats in the synagogues ⁷ and greetings in the marketplaces and being called rabbi by others.** This man is a picture of many in the church. Everyone who sees them thinks they are pure, holy and righteous. They have convinced everyone they are the epitome of righteousness, holiness and virtue. They have even convinced themselves they are right and everyone around them who is not exactly like them is wrong. What a pity!

The other man who came to pray that day was a publican or tax collector. He was a spiritual outcast. While he was welcome to come to the Temple to pray in the Court of the Jews, he would not have been allowed to attend the meetings at the synagogue. The other Jews hated and looked down on him. He was a tax collector. He worked for Rome, the nation that dominated and ruled Israel at the time. Rome collected three kinds of taxes from the people she conquered. They collected land, head tax, and a custom tax. These taxes were collected in a three-tiered system. In this system, Rome levied the taxes. They were collected by a chief tax collector (i.e. Zacchaeus.) who controlled the work of several tax collectors (i.e. Matthew).

The chief tax collector would pay Rome for a certain area or district which gave him the authority to collect the taxes there. He would in turn sub-lease that area to tax collectors. The chief tax collector could set his own rates and the men who worked for him could set their own rates. As a result, Rome received its taxes, by the chief tax collectors while the local tax collectors grew wealthy from extorting large sums of money from the common people. A tax collector was known for his greed and dishonesty. He was viewed as a traitor to Israel and not even worthy of compassion or concern from the Jews.

This man is a picture of others we find in the church. I refer to them as the "others" because this is what most of those in attendance call them. These are the people who do not act like we think they should. They might not dress like we think they should. They might not do things and say things like we think they should. Like the publican, these people are in the church often looked down on by the people who think they are more spiritual.

Both of these men went to the Temple to pray. When they opened their mouths and began to speak, the true character of their heart is put on display. As it turns out, you really cannot judge a book by its cover. The man everyone thought was righteous was really a hypocrite, while the Lord accepted the man everyone looked down on.

Join me in the examination of the prayers of these two men today. Their words and attitudes have something to teach us about how we should approach the Lord in sincere prayer. This parable is also a lesson on how we should see others. When the Pharisee begins to pray, he is quick to tell the Lord how things really are. He brags about his righteousness by comparing himself to other men. He even sees the Publican praying nearby and talks about how much better he is than him.

William Barclay records the following. "It is on record that Rabbi Simeon ben Jocai once said, "If there are only two righteous men in the world, I and my son are these two; if there is only one, I am he!" The Pharisee did not really go to pray; he went to inform God how good he was thereby making him guilty of showing us an example of the wrong way to pray. He brags about his religious works. He brags about his giving. He tells the Lord how great he is and how well he is doing.

It was common for the Pharisees to stand when they prayed. They would spread their arms, lift their voices as loud as they could and launch into long, complicated, self-serving prayer. He appears to be talking to the Lord when, in truth, he is only talking to himself. His prayer got no higher than the roof of his mouth.

Let's take a closer look at the publican who knew he had nothing at all to offer the Lord. He knew he was a wicked sinner. When he prays, there is no pride, pretense, or any hint of self-righteousness. He makes no attempts to justify himself or his lifestyle in the eyes of the Lord. He just humbles himself before God, tells the truth, and asks for mercy. He would not even lift his eyes toward heaven. The Bible says, he beats himself on the breast, knowing his real problem was a problem of the heart. The Pharisee, on the other hand is blissfully unaware anything is wrong in his heart. His prayer is short, simple and to the point. We could learn a lot from this man and his style of prayer!

Let me offer a few thoughts on how the prayers of these two men teach us about prayer. The prayer of the Pharisee was indicative of the praying of most self-righteous Jews in that era. Here are a few of the problems that crept into prayer in Jesus' day and even still today.

1. **Prayer had become nothing more than a ritual.** The Jew prayed, but his prayers were scripted and the form was set. He either quoted them from memory or read them. Now before you say to yourself, "Wow, that is a good way to pray", don't." There was nothing good about these prayers. The Jews prayed faithfully morning, noon, and night.

Every morning and evening, faithful Jews would repeat one of two prayers the *Shema* and the *Shemoneh 'esray*. The *Shema* prayer was formed from selected phrases from Deuteronomy 6:4-9; 11: 13-21 and

Numbers 15:37-41. Often, the Shema was used in its abbreviated form. This would be just Deuteronomy 6:4 (ESV) [4] "Hear, O Israel: The LORD our God, the LORD is one.

Another prayer they prayed was called the *Shemoneh 'esray*, which means *The Eighteen*. This was a series of eighteen prayers that addressed various aspects of life. The faithful Jew would pray all eighteen of these prayers three times every day. Regardless of where the Jew was, at the third, sixth or ninth hour, he would stop what he was doing and offer the necessary prayers. Of course, some could have been praying sincerely, but most were simply following ritual.

2. **Predetermined prayers were formulated for every aspect of life**. Every conceivable turn of life has a prayer developed to deal with it. This also led to prayer being something that could be recited from the head and not lifted up from the spirit. This is why I warn those who read books with pre-scripted prayers in them to use them correctly. Those are only seeds to help you to develop your thoughts as you approach the throne of God. Even in the books I write, the prewritten prayers are only a starting point, not a stopping point. My desire is as you read my words and the Word, the Holy Spirit will speak to you and direct you in your prayer.

3. **Prayer was limited to preset times and occasions**. Instead of praying when they felt led to, or when a need arose, they only

pray at set times. There are still religious groups who do this today. We need to remember there is nothing wrong with praying at a predetermined time. The problem is if this is the only time(s) you pray. The Bible tells us to be in an attitude of prayer always. Remember **1 Thessalonians 5:17. Pray without ceasing.**

4. **Long prayers were held in high regard**. The Jews believed the longer and more elaborate the prayer, the more likely it was to be heard by God. Jesus warned against this practice in **Matthew 6:7.** **[7] "And when you pray, do not heap up empty phrases as the Gentiles do, for they think that they will be heard for their many words.** Nothing wrong with long-winded praying as long as the Spirit is moving in it. But when a person prays a long time to impress others, they have crossed the line into pretense. I want to repeat long prayers are okay when the Holy Spirit is the driving force. I am not giving you a license to judge the heart of anyone's prayers. I want you to take a look at your current prayer routine.

5. **Many prayers were comprised of meaningless repetition**. The Jews were notorious for repeating phrases and adding adjectives to the name of God, thinking they would be heard by Him. This was a pagan practice that, sadly, is found in some Christian circles today.

6. **The desire to be seen and heard of others.** This is the worst offense of all. Prayer had ceased to be about communion with God and degenerated into an attempt to impress others. This is the attitude Jesus is dealing with in these verses.

Unfortunately, many of these same problems have crept into the prayer life of many of our churches. Both of these men went to the house of prayer. Both of these men stood in the place where God promised to hear His people when they prayed. Most Christians can quote **2 Chronicles 7:13-14** which says, [13] **When I shut up the heavens so that there is no rain, or command the locust to devour the land, or send pestilence among my people,** [14] **if my people who are called by my name humble themselves, and pray and seek my face and turn from their wicked ways, then I will hear from heaven and will forgive their sin and heal their land.** However, most who quote verses 13-14 are not as familiar with verse 15, where God promises, **"Now my eyes will be open and my ears attentive to the prayer that is made in this place."**

Both of these men prayed, but the outcome was different for each of them. One man got everything; the other got nothing! One man came in confident while the other came in convicted. The Lord heard the wicked, sinful, hated Publican. God heard his simple prayer and received him. His sins were forgiven, and he went to his house justified in the eyes of the Lord. The Pharisee, on the other hand, was ignored by the Lord. As I mentioned a few minutes ago, he was just praying to himself. He went home feeling good about himself. He went home sure he was right with the Lord, when he was actually still lost in his sins. Did you notice in the beginning Jesus told this parable to the Pharisees? He wanted these self-righteous hypocrites to understand the way up in the eyes of the Lord is down.

The way to be honored by the Lord is to realize you are nothing before the Lord.

The way to forgiveness is through confession of sin.

The way to be right with the Lord is to realize just how wrong we are.

Jesus wanted them to know we should never be in the business of judging others, but we should be in the business of judging ourselves, **¹⁴ I tell you, this man went down to his house justified, rather than the other. For everyone who exalts himself will be humbled, but the one who humbles himself will be exalted."**

Jesus wanted them to know they were not to focus their attention on the lives of others, but they were to worry about their own walk with the Lord, **⁹ He also told this parable to some who trusted in themselves that they were righteous, and treated others with contempt.**

We are all guilty of this from time to time. We all have those little areas of irritation that don't bother us when we see it in our lives.

It only bothers us when we see it or hear about it in the lives of those around us. If we are not careful, we will become like the Pharisees and come to despise other people. If we are not careful, we will think our way is the only way and anyone who is not like us is not worth the time of day.

Jesus wanted to open the eyes of the Pharisees to the truth that people around them needed to know the Lord. Even the people they despised needed to know about the Lord. Here are some things to prompt your prayer today.

I have no business judging someone just because they don't do everything like I do it. I should pray for them and be an example of love and light to them. I should never judge them.

When I am like the Pharisees, I prove I am nothing like Jesus. He doesn't despise the sinner; He loves and works to bring about change in his life, **¹⁷ Therefore, if anyone is in Christ, he is a new creation. The old has passed away; behold, the new has come. 2 Corinthians 5:17**

Some people have been given more light than others. This is just the truth and God's prerogative. If this is you, right and wrong is not lost to you. You are responsible for the knowledge you carry. There will be people you come in contact with who have not journeyed as far down the road of faith. What do they need? They need patience, love and guidance. They need someone who will demonstrate the love of Christ to them and help them to reach their full potential in Jesus. The last thing they need is judgment.

Allow me to share one last thing about this parable Jesus taught. One man went to church and left with nothing. He went through the rituals. He judged others by his standards. He prayed his self-serving prayers. He worshiped himself. This man went home feeling good about himself, but He received nothing from God for his efforts. The other man went to church and left with everything. He didn't make a spiritual show. He prayed a simple prayer. He offered God honesty, confession and worship. He left church right with the Lord.

There is a major difference between the two. The difference was in the attitude and condition of their hearts. One was full of himself and thought he needed nothing more. The other knew he was nothing and possessed nothing. He humbled himself before God and he was blessed. Which one are you? Do you look down on those who don't know as much Bible as you? Do you judge people who haven't grown spiritually as much as you think you have? Do you listen to the sermon picturing people the message applies to other than you? Are you resting on your own laurels? How will what we discovered together change the way you come to church, virtually or in person?

7 A PRAYER FOR DIFFICULT DAYS

[32]Now when Mary came to where Jesus was and saw him, she fell at his feet, saying to him, "Lord, if you had been here, my brother would not have died." [33]When Jesus saw her weeping, and the Jews who had come with her also weeping, he was deeply moved in his spirit and greatly troubled. [34]And he said, "Where have you laid him?" They said to him, "Lord, come and see." [35]Jesus wept. [36] So the Jews said, "See how he loved him!" [37]But some of them said, "Could not he who opened the eyes of the blind man also have kept this man from dying?" [38] Then Jesus, deeply moved again, came to the tomb. It was a cave, and a stone lay against it. [39] Jesus said, "Take away the stone." Martha, the sister of the dead man, said to him, "Lord, by this time there will be an odor, for he has been dead four days." [40] Jesus said to her, "Did I not tell you that if you believed you would see the glory of God?" [41]So they took away the stone. And Jesus lifted up his eyes and said, "Father, I thank you that you have heard me. [42] I knew that you always hear me, but I said this on account of the people standing around, that they may believe that you sent me." [43]When he had said these things, he cried out with a loud voice, "Lazarus, come out." [44] The man who had died came out, his hands and feet bound with linen strips, and his face wrapped with a cloth. Jesus said to them, "Unbind him, and let him go." John 11:32-44

It's easy to blame God when life goes wrong. He can do anything. Stop anything. Change anything. But sometimes He does not. The world is full of death and disease and destruction and sin. Bad things happen to good people...even good Christian people.

God never promised I would get what I want, that my days would be easy, that just because I chose to follow Him I would not suffer, sorrow and taste the salt of my tears, or that He would let me skip the heavy season, the hard season and the horrible season. And that Ladies and Gentlemen is where the greatest source of our disappointment comes from.

When I look at our devotional reading, I am reminded of something my predecessor Pastor C. C. Cooper, whom I was blessed to serve as his Joshua and he as my Moses for over 5 year, would often remind me. True peace will always find me when I give thanks in the worst of situations. I'm still here, still living, not destroyed, not consumed, even when people and situations have tried to break me.

I can still hear those saints that shaped, shared and spurred me in my spiritual maturity and ministry, many who are gone on to be with Jesus used to sing a song entitled, "In the Garden" and it went like this:

I come to the garden alone,

While the dew is still on the roses,

And the voice I hear falling on my ear,

The Son of God discloses...

And He walks with me, and He talks with me,

And He tells me I am His own,

And the joy we share as we tarry there,

None other, has ever, known!

I remember the times He walked me through the darkness of feeling alone and abandoned. Has He done it for you? There were times when it looked bad and bleak, but we made it another year.

As my perspective changes, so does my disappointment. God's purpose is not to keep me wrapped in that bubble and keep me away from the harsh realities of the world. It is to walk with me through them. His purpose is to refine my faith.

This is one of the most amazing passages in the entire Bible, I believe! Here we are allowed to see the glory, power and majesty of the Christ's power in a dazzling display. Here we see a man named Lazarus, a friend of Jesus and one whom He had spent many nights within his home! Lazarus also had two sisters who adored and honored Jesus, named Mary and Martha.

In this text, we see what Jesus did for Lazarus. We also see what He can do for the person who is lost and in sin today. This passage shows us how Jesus can take you from worry to worship; from crying to celebrating, and from pouting to praising. If you do not know the Lord, or if your situation looks dismal, dark, and even dead, this would be a great day to come to Him by faith. If you do know Him, it would be a great time to remember what He did for you when He saved you by His grace.

Let's dive into this passage. There will be times when the conditions of our lives will be more than we could ever imagine. A message is sent to Jesus from Lazarus' sisters. **So the sisters sent to him, saying, "Lord, he whom you love is ill." John 11:3 (ESV)**

When we arrive at **John 11:17** we find these words. **Jesus found that Lazarus had already been in the tomb four days**. **John 11:21** says, **Martha said "Lord, my brother would not have died. In John 11:32 Mary said "Lord, if you had been here, my brother would not have died."** Lazarus' situation mirrored that of someone lost in sin. **Ephesians 2:1** says, **"And you were dead in the trespasses and sins."** In a dead condition, you cannot sense the presence of the Lord. You cannot respond to the things of God. You cannot enjoy fellowship with God. You are dead and in a pitiful condition.

39 Jesus said, "Take away the stone." Martha, the sister of the dead man, said to him, "Lord, by this time there will be an odor, for he has been dead four days" When Jesus arrived at his tomb, he had been dead for four days. He had been dead long enough to stink. This is an accurate picture of sinners! The lost person may be good and moral, but if they are lost, they are dead. Some have signs of their lost condition. They may curse, get drunk in excess or live a morally unclean lifestyle. They, too, are dead in trespasses and sins. Then there are the hardcore sinners. They are lost and they make no excuses for it. They have the stench of sin all around them! They are dead and everyone knows it! I must say to you, there are no degrees of dead, only degrees of decay! And just as the physically dead are good for nothing but to be buried, the spiritually dead are fit for nothing but Hell.

As you listen to Martha, Mary and the others talking about Lazarus, you get the idea they have given up on him. In their minds, he is dead and nothing more can be done about it. Had this been any other cemetery, I might have agreed with them. But there was one subtle difference that day, Jesus Christ was there! The others may have been ready to leave Lazarus in the grave, but Jesus was not! He makes all the difference! Jesus is the only One who can make a difference in a person who is dead in sin and headed to Hell! If Jesus had not passed by where Lazarus was, he would have rotted in that grave! Ladies and gentlemen, boys and girls, I need to sound a warning right here. You and I can try any method we choose, but if the Lord Jesus Christ does not bring life to our dead souls, we will remain dead.

Can I talk to the mother or father who feels their son or daughter has been gone too long and too far? Tell Jesus. Let me talk to that spouse who has rehearsed the hurt and is headed to divorce court. Tell Jesus. Maybe there is a friendship on the verge of ending, tell Jesus. We may give up on folks like this crowd did with Lazarus, but thank God, Jesus doesn't operate like we do! When it looked like there was no hope, the Lord came to where Lazarus lay in darkness and He changed everything for Him! What has He done for you? What do you need Him to do?

When the Lord Jesus called out to the tomb, His call was personal. In verses 42-43 He says, **42 "I knew that you always hear me, but I said this on account of the people standing around, that they may believe that you sent me." 43 When he had said these things, he cried out with a loud voice, "Lazarus, come out.** "Jesus called specifically for Lazarus to come out of the tomb! That call was for no one else that day. It was a call designed for one man and one man alone! The Gospel call is not a general call to all men as many have misinterpreted! No, the call of salvation is a call to individuals from a holy God. I know the Bible says, *"whosoever will"* may be saved. **(Romans 10:13)** However, I also know the call of the Lord is an intensely personal call! When He comes calling for you, He will come to you as an individual. When He comes, He will come for you personally! How many of us can testify to that truth?

The call was very clear that day for Lazarus. Jesus told Lazarus exactly what to do! When He comes calling, there will be no doubt as to what He wants you to do! When He comes calling, His call will be for you to come to Him. His call will be for you to believe in Him by faith. His call will be a call to repent of your sins and turn to Jesus for salvation.

This call was a powerful call for Lazarus. It brought him out of death and darkness into light and life! It changed everything for him forever. When Jesus calls you and you heed the call, it has the power and potential to change your life forever! His call has the power to penetrate the blindness of sin and awaken the lost person to his need for the Lord. His call is a painful thing, but it is necessary, and in the end, it turns out to be a blessed thing because it leads to salvation! Check out verse 44. **The man who had died came out, his hands and feet bound with linen strips, and his face wrapped with a cloth. Jesus said to them, "Unbind him, and let him go."**

Here is a man who has been dead for four days, and at Jesus' command, He is alive! He is able to meet with and embrace his family and friends. He is able to have fellowship with those he loves again! He is alive! Hallelujah!

Now before we move into complete celebration, I must go back and talk about the point at which Lazarus came alive. It was not when he walked out the tomb, for he was still bound. Notice Jesus has to tell those around him to set him free from his bindings. In those bindings, Lazarus still looked like a dead man. With those bindings, he was still in bondage. Jesus wanted to illustrate to us how we must participate in our resurrection. Yes, He has made us alive, but there are still many of us walking around in our bindings and even stinking.

Is this you? Are you unaware of what total freedom looks like because you are still bound by the bandages of your past? Are you still bound because of hurt? Jesus has called your name specifically to come forth. Why are you still walking around bound?

Lazarus had spent four days in a tomb, totally oblivious to his condition. Now he is alive and sitting at a table, fellowshipping with the Lord Jesus Christ! Everything changed for this man! Has Jesus Christ ever showed up at the tomb of your life and called you to come to Him? Did you go when He called? Or, are you still trapped in the darkness, lost and lingering? If you need salvation, and Jesus is calling you, please come to Him. If your relationship with Him needs work, then please come before Him and do what He is speaking to your heart!

8 A PRAYER OF FEASTING IN THE MIDST OF FAMINE

13 But now I am coming to you, and these things I speak in the world, that they may have my joy fulfilled in themselves. 14 I have given them your word, and the world has hated them because they are not of the world, just as I am not of the world. 15 I do not ask that you take them out of the world, but that you keep them from the evil one. 16 They are not of the world, just as I am not of the world. 17 Sanctify them in the truth; your word is truth. 18 As you sent me into the world, so I have sent them into the world. 19 And for their sake I consecrate myself, that they also may be sanctified in truth. 20 "I do not ask for these only, but also for those who will believe in me through their word, 21 that they may all be one, just as you, Father, are in me, and I in you, that they also may be in us, so that the world may believe that you have sent me. John 17:13-21

At the time this book is being written, we are in a global pandemic. I have come to realize the things I need and the things I can do without. I do not have to go out to eat. I do not have to spend money unnecessarily. I do not need an audience to proclaim the Gospel of Jesus Christ. I do need daily communion with God. I do need fellowship with the body of Christ. More importantly, I need the Word of God.

"John Knox, on his death-bed in 1572, asked his wife to read to him John 17, 'where', he said, 'I cast my first anchor.'" (Bruce)

The Bible is filled with prayers. There is the prayer of Solomon **(1 Kings 8)**, the prayer of Abraham **(Genesis 18)**, Hannah's prayer **(I Samuel 2)**, and Moses' prayer **(Exodus 32)**. The prayer I want to introduce today is the prayer of Jesus. In the book of John chapter 17, we find Jesus praying. John makes reference to the fact Jesus is praying at 'the hour'. It's the hour when Jesus would bring glory to His Father and He wanted to make sure the divine timetable was completed. Why did Jesus pray? Was it a sign of weakness? Not at all. Jesus prayed because His Father would not be glorified if His sacrifice was unacceptable.

Notice Jesus' posture. It is not the posture many of us have been taught to get into during our prayer time. What does the preacher often say? "Bow your heads and close your eyes." The preacher may even say, "If you are able, get down on your knees." However, Jesus did neither of those things, He looked upward. Jesus was in a posture of hope and confidence in the One He was praying. This is an element of prayer I feel so many have lost. We pray, and yet do not have the faith, hope, or confidence in God when amen is uttered. Without faith in God, what is the purpose of praying? Is it because you have not conceded to His will? Is it because the only answer you will accept is the one where God does exactly as you say? The next time you pray, I would encourage you to remind yourself to whom you are praying. That should definitely jumpstart your faith.

Let's get back to Jesus. He began by praying for Himself and then began to pray for His disciples and concluded the prayer by praying for those who would be saved from the disciples' witness. Yes, over 2000 years ago, Jesus prayed for you and me. He had us on His mind and more importantly in His heart. So, what did Jesus pray for us?

Before I answer the aforementioned question, I have a question for you. What is your greatest possession? In my possession I have the Bible of the late Dr. C. C. Cooper. I also have the Official Manual of the Church of God in Christ left to me by my grandfather, the late Elder Joseph Jackson Gaddis. I treasure both of the gifts because of who they belonged to. Jesus prays to His Father saying, "I have given them your Word…" **(v. 14)** Why would Jesus make reference to this fact?

Jesus makes this statement for us to realize the true value of the Word of God. We have in our possession, not just words printed in a book with a leather or hardback cover. We have in our possession not just words regurgitated by a preacher. **2 Timothy 3:16** tells us, **All Scripture is breathed out by God and profitable for teaching, for reproof, for correction, and for training in righteousness.** It is a gift given to us by Jesus who received it from His Father. It is a gift from heaven. This is why we must never take the Word of God for granted. When we take the Word of God for granted, we become distant from God and detached from His glory. When we take the Word of God for granted, we become stifled by deceit and surrounded by darkness. When we take the Word of God for granted, we become poisoned with pride and penetrated with pretense. I could go on, but I am sure you get the point.

There is grave danger in neglecting the Word of God. D. L. Moody said, "This book will keep you from sin or sin will keep you from the book." It is the Word of God that provides light in darkness **(Psalm 119:105)**. It is the Word of God that gives us assurance of God's love. **(John 3:16, Romans 5:8)** It is the Word of God that is nourishment for our soul. **(Hebrews 5:12-14)** It is the Word of God that gives us strength and security. **(Luke 6:47-48)** Why would anyone ever neglect the Word of God? Just as we receive the gift of salvation, we also receive the gift of God's Word.

So, now that you understand the danger of neglecting the Word of God, I want to expound more on the deliverance from the necessity of the Word of God. When your mind learns the truth of God's Word then your heart will love God's truth through the Son. And furthermore, you will begin to yield to the Holy Spirit and live God's truth. Learning and loving should always lead to living. (**Romans 12:1-2).** Your belief should dictate your behavior. Your actions and attitude should match your altitude. **(Colossians 3:1-2)**

It is because of our knowledge of the Word of God that the world hates us. They hate us because as we learn the Word of God and live it out, the less we conform. The enemy would rather we prioritize the things of this world and live according to our sinful nature. He is okay with us lying, cheating, not forgiving others, holding grudges, gossiping and stepping on others to get ahead. He does not want us to seek first the kingdom of God and His righteousness. **(Matthew 6:33)**.

Ever wonder why there are times you feel like you don't fit in? The reason is simple. You are not of this world. During the earthly ministry of Jesus, He was not liked at all. As a matter of fact, He was hated. Now I know hate is a strong word and you may be asking why people would hate me just for possessing the gift of God's Word.

Because the more you read the Word of God, the more you grow to love God. The more you love God, the less you look like the world. It is through the hearing of God's Word and your love for His Son, you become a true doer of the Word.

Have you achieved that moment like Jeremiah, when the Word was unto me the joy and rejoicing of my heart"? **(Jeremiah 15:16)** Or maybe, you have felt like the Psalmist who wrote, "I rejoice in Thy Word, as on that findeth great spoil." **(Psalm 119:162)** Both Jeremiah and the Psalmist understood the point I truly want you to receive in your heart today. The Word of God is a treasure. Through the Word of God, we are exposed to the reality of the world's deception and dangerous devices. We also experience the revelation of the sufficiency and security of God through the Word.

With that being said, you are probably wondering what I should glean from Jesus's prayer to His Father. The answer is found in **verse 17. "Sanctify them in the truth; your word is truth."** I don't know about you, but sometimes I pray for God just to bring me on home. The longer I live, the darker this world becomes. In this current season, I feel we have digressed instead of progressed in America. Then I remember I have been set apart. When you and I were saved we were set apart for God.

The word sanctification comes from the root word, sanctify. It means to "set apart for the intended use of the designer". Let me see if I can make this definition a little clearer. A car is sanctified when it is driven, not when it is sitting on a car lot. A chair is sanctified when it is sat on, not when it is being used to stand on to reach something. A pencil is sanctified when it is being used to write, not when it is in the pencil box.

The biblical definition for sanctify is "to make holy". Christians are sanctified when we are living out our divine purpose. **For we are his workmanship, created in Christ Jesus for good works, which God prepared beforehand, that we should walk in them. (Ephesians 2:10)** Does it surprise you to know God created you to do His will? Maybe this fact makes you anxious. No need to be anxious because sanctification is all God's work. **Every good gift and every perfect gift is from above. (James 1:17)**

While sanctification is all God's work, we do play a part. We must internalize the Word of God. We must get to know what pleases God and what hurts God's heart. We must hide it in our hearts that we might not sin against God. Just as we need a daily dose of vitamins to live a healthy physical life, we need a daily dose of God's Word to live a healthy spiritual life. We cannot pick and choose the passages we can do easily and lay aside the ones that are more difficult. You know, the ones our flesh still craves. Children crave sweets, but what parent allows sweets to be the only part of their daily nutrition? No good parent does.

So, as God's children, we are to eat the Word of God every day. We must allow it to digest. Chew it up and not swallow it whole. Some of it may need to be eaten in smaller bites. And then wash it down with prayer. Jesus understood some of it may be difficult to digest. This is the reason He became our great intercessor. Jesus understands what this world is like. He knows the evil that exists. He knows we will be tempted to sin. He knows at times we will sin. And each and every time we do, He whispers to His Father, "I covered that." Aren't you glad!

Jesus did not only pray for us to be sanctified in the truth, He also prayed that **we all would be one just as you, Father, are in me, and I in you, that they also may be in us, so that the world may believe that you have sent me. (v.21)**

Division in the body of Christ, hurts our witness. It is not a good representation of Jesus and the change we claim He has made in our lives. When we are out of fellowship with one another, it is an indication of the sin we continue to let rule our lives. It is evidence of us practicing sin. It is evidence we have not turned the problem over to God. It is an external display of the darkness in our hearts. Whether you believe it or accept it, all Christians are a part of God's family. That fact makes them apart of your family.

The Puritan preacher Thomas Brooks wrote: "Discord and division become no Christian. For wolves to worry the lambs is no wonder, but for one lamb to worry another, this is unnatural and monstrous." Be Transformed (John 13-21).

Understand this, the unity Jesus is speaking of is not of uniformity. Jesus is speaking of unity in God and the purposes of God. In other words, Christians should work together to glorify God and expand His kingdom. There is no such thing as not being able to work with someone in kingdom business. There is no such thing as intentionally sabotaging someone else's efforts to do the work of the Lord. And yet, after pastoring for twenty-nine years, I have seen this very thing.

Hebrews 12:1-2 says, **Therefore, since we are surrounded by so great a cloud of witnesses, let us also lay aside every weight, and sin which clings so closely, and let us run with endurance the race that is set before us, [2] looking to Jesus, the founder and perfecter of our faith, who for the joy that was set before him endured the cross, despising the shame, and is seated at the right hand of the throne of God.** Allow me to give you a few examples of the weight the writer of Hebrew was referencing. He was referring to the weight of unforgiveness, grudges, strife, and unholy speech. He was telling us to throw off **sexual immorality, impurity, sensuality, idolatry, sorcery, enmity, strife, jealousy, fits of anger, rivalries, dissensions, divisions, envy, drunkenness, orgies, and things like these. (Galatians 5:19-21)** These things hinder the work of God. We must also remember any work done without a true heart for God, devoid of all these things, is not received by God.

Work for Christ should be full of **love, joy, peace, patience, kindness, goodness, faithfulness, gentleness, and self-control. (Galatians 5:22-23)** God does not care about our personal likes and dislikes when it comes to His will. I was thinking about the diversity of the twelve disciples. There were fishermen, a tax collector, a zealot, and a variety of tradesmen. They may not have had anything in common before saying yes to follow Jesus. Jesus, however, became their commonality once He made them a disciple.

I have a question for you. What excuse do you think you can tell God for not walking in unity with your brother or sister in Christ? What excuse do you feel God will accept? I will answer the questions for you. There is not one. God does not accept our excuses for not following His will. It is a requirement for being a true child of God. Jesus did not lash out when He knew the Pharisees and Sadducees were talking about Him and plotting against Him. Jesus did not ask His disciples to separate the 5000 men, not counting women and children, by those who would scream, "Crucify him! Crucify him!" No, He simply told His disciples to separate them in groups of twelve. Jesus did not revoke the healing of the nine lepers when only the one came back and said thank you. Jesus did not only wash ten of the disciples' feet in the Upper Room. He included Peter who would deny Him and

Judas who would betray Him. He even performed major surgery on one of the guards who came to arrest Him. Jesus performed a mighty miracle in the midst of the madness. Jesus went about His Father's business in spite of what He faced.

Our effectiveness is only as good as our unity. A choir is made up of sopranos, altos, tenors, and bass. A good choir is one who can blend. A football team is made up of different players with different races, weight, and backgrounds. Nevertheless, when they become a part of the team, they have one goal, crossing the goal line. If the players are working against one another this will not be achieved. If the blockers do not block for the quarterback, he can be injured. Some players are more gifted than others. Some can play both offense and defense. Some players only practice and never play. The good news is when they win the championship game, every player receives a Super Bowl ring.

The body of Christ is made up the same way. Within the body of Christ there are men and women, all nationalities, varying gifts. If one individual does not do what he or she has been created to do it hinders the expansion of the kingdom of God. If one person refuses to work together, tears down another member, sabotages kingdom efforts, God is not pleased. My heart is saddened right now as I write this because the state of our world has exposed the problems of the church. I am not speaking only of the church universal; I am speaking of the church I am privileged to Pastor also. My dialogue with the pastors who are covered in my ministry, Praying for our Pastors, has revealed to me, I am not alone.

We must always remember God is not surprised by anything that happens. He allows these things to happen to see if you have grown spiritually. He is not concerned about the one you will not forgive; His concern is with you. He is not concerned with the one you continue to dig ditches for, He is concerned with you who claim to love Him. He is concerned with your commitment to Him. He is concerned with your dedication to Him. He wants to know if you can lay aside your feelings and follow Him faithfully. He wants to know if you can put down your grudge and give generously of yourself to service. Will you depend on Him to fight your battle or will you continue to disappoint Him with your behavior? In this time in history, God is looking for His true believers, those who will worship Him in spirit and in truth.

Your disunity in the body of Christ will affect the presence of God and His power in your prayer life. Your disunity in the body of Christ will cause a good idea that could have yielded much fruit to be fruitless. Your disunity in the body of Christ will be evident to those around you. Those who are members of the body of Christ see you not speaking and not supporting. There are unbelievers who observe your behavior, overhear your conversations and say, "There is no point in me becoming a Christian if this is an example of what a relationship with Christ looks like." They visit our churches and hear you tearing down members of our families. They join our churches and leave because they connect with individuals with vendettas and personal agendas.

This is serious. Progress is hindered by disunity. Jesus realized how serious unity in the body of Christ would be and went to His Father on our behalf. Jesus prayed we would be as unified as him and His Father. He prayed we would be unified in our nature, character, and purpose. And God always answers the prayers of His Son. Let me say that again. God always answers the prayers of His Son. This means change is possible, but God will not force you. It is not a matter of cannot for a child of God. It is a matter of will not. **I can do all things through Christ who strengthens me** applies here as well. **(Philippians 4:13)** When true unity is present, God's glory is on display. We become a billboard for Christ. We become a walking advertisement for kingdom building. It is bigger than us. It is bigger than petty differences and personality clashes. Through our unity souls are saved.

I want to end this day with a few questions.

Will you be committed to a daily diet of the Word of God?

Will you allow the Word of God to penetrate your hardened heart?

Will you allow the Word of God to be your only guiding force?

Will you allow the Word of God to show you the way to becoming one with your brother and sister in Christ as Jesus and the Father are one?

8 A PRAYER FOR DIVINE ENABLEMENT

---

23 When they were released, they went to their friends and reported what the chief priests and the elders had said to them. 24 And when they heard it, they lifted their voices together to God and said, "Sovereign Lord, who made the heaven and the earth and the sea and everything in them, 25 who through the mouth of our father David, your servant,[a] said by the Holy Spirit,

> *"Why did the Gentiles rage,*
> *and the peoples plot in vain?*
> *26 The kings of the earth set themselves,*
> *and the rulers were gathered together,*
> *against the Lord and against his Anointed'[b]——*

27 for truly in this city there were gathered together against your holy servant Jesus, whom you anointed, both Herod and Pontius Pilate, along with the Gentiles and the peoples of Israel, 28 to do whatever your hand and your plan had predestined to take place. 29 And now, Lord, look upon their threats and grant to your servants to continue to speak your word with all boldness, 30 while you stretch out your hand to heal, and signs and wonders are performed through the name of your holy servant Jesus." 31 And when they had prayed, the place in which they were gathered together was shaken, and they were all filled with the Holy Spirit and continued to speak the word of God with boldness. Acts 4:23-31

John Knox was a sixteenth century reformer. He boldly spoke the truth to his large congregation in Scotland but was arrested for it and chained to the oars of a ship. During long months of pulling on oars, he built not only his physical strength but also strength of fervent prayer. His cry was, "O God! Give me Scotland or I die!" His life and his work for God became so powerful the Queen of Scotland is quoted as saying, "I fear the prayers of John Knox more than all the assembled armies of Europe."

This same story could be told of Daniel in the days of captivity in Babylon. In Daniel 6 the nation of Judah is in captivity. Daniel is working for King Darius. He is positioned for a promotion and the other king's administrators become jealous. They knew Daniel worshiped another God and convinced the king to put an ordinance in place that would punish Daniel if he continued to worship his God. So, what did Daniel do? With full knowledge of the ordinance, he returned to his room and continued praying as he had always done. The king had no choice but to throw Daniel in the lions' den.

After being thrown in the lions' den, King Darius told Daniel to call out for his God. Through the life Daniel led, even the king recognized Daniel's God was living, active and powerful. Daniel exhibited spiritual boldness even though it meant being in direct opposition to the highest court in the land. His act was so great the king made a powerful declaration to the people of Persia.

[25] Then King Darius wrote to all the nations and peoples of every language in all the earth:

"May you prosper greatly

[26] "I issue a decree that in every part of my kingdom people must fear and reverence the God of Daniel.

"For he is the living God
    and he endures forever;
his kingdom will not be destroyed,
    his dominion will never end.
[27] He rescues and he saves;
    he performs signs and wonders
    in the heavens and on the earth.
He has rescued Daniel
    from the power of the lions."
[28] So Daniel prospered during the reign of Darius and the reign of Cyrus the Persian. (Daniel 6:25-28)

Why did I share these two stories with you? A true believer will suffer. Today suffering looks like slander, gossip, abuse, exclusion, or violence. It can happen at home, on social media, and even in the church. Your suffering may be private or public. It can be at the hands of one individual or a group of individuals. You will be tempted to quit. Your attitude may be that your life was so much better before you said yes to God. The story in today's text encourages us not to quit no matter what.

Today's text we find Peter and John were being released after being thrown in jail for healing a man. As a stipulation of their release, the chief priests and elders commanded them to no longer preach in the name of Jesus. Upon release they told their friends about the order and immediately their friends began to pray. Now, I need to pause right here and stress to you the importance of having praying friends. You may have drinking, smoking, gossiping and partying buddies, but if you don't have yourself a group of friends who will intercede on your behalf you are missing out.

What did the people pray? They began by acknowledging God for who He is. He is the Creator of everything. Our prayers should always begin with admiration for our Father. They went on to acknowledge the sovereignty of God. They understood everything that happened was because God allowed it to happen. Our prayers would probably be different if they were devoid of complaining about our circumstances and instead asking God what the lesson is, we should learn. They understood that even the suffering was a part of God's sovereign will.

The third piece to the prayer was asking God to grant His servants to continue to speak the Word with boldness. They did not pray strike down the chief priests and elders. They didn't ask to be removed from the place of persecution. They planted their feet and asked God not to let anything get in the way of doing His will. **"And now, Lord, look upon their threats and grant to your servants to continue to speak your word with all boldness." (v. 29)** Their attitude was not one of defeat but determination. They didn't scatter in fear, no they prayed for strength. They did not whine to God while worrying about the consequences of not following the command. Instead they worshipped God and waited for His answer.

That is precisely what we are called to do. When God has given us an assignment, nothing should hinder our progress. We must have an unwavering conviction. We must obey God no matter what may be lurking around the corner. Our job is to be obedient. Notice what Peter and John's friends prayed. Their prayer was for God to allow His spokesmen to be even bolder in their witness. They prayed God would continue to heal and show Himself strong through His servants.

Notice there was not any jealousy among the friends. Notice they understood their place in the grand scheme of things. They didn't get in a corner and decide who the next leaders should be. They didn't begin to discuss how they could have done things better and not be foolish enough to speak truth to power. No, their only concern was for the name of Jesus to be lifted high.

The conviction these individuals had was of God's power and their own futility. These things had not been happening in their name, but only in the name of Jesus. I often chuckle at individuals who believe success is dependent upon their presence and support. We must get to the place in our Christian journey where we can acknowledge like Paul that nothing good is in us and every good thing comes from God. **(Romans 7:18, James 1:17)** We also must get to the place where we understand God's gifts cannot be manufactured. Yes, you may be able to do the same thing and even receive support from others. The difference is a true gift from God produces godly fruit. A true gift from God creates Christ followers and not our disciples. When your gift comes from God someone else can step on the scene and you not feel threatened by what they have to offer. You welcome them in and see how your gifts may be used together to benefit the kingdom of God. Remember, it was Jesus who prayed in John 17, "that all of them may be one, Father, just as you are in me and I am in you." **(v.21)** There is no sign of Peter and John being puffed up. They exhibited great humility. Peter and John's only concern was to encourage and edify the believers.

Is that your only concern? When you do things in church is your strongest desire to encourage and edify others? Do you continue to serve in spite of the whispers and negativity you encounter? When you serve are you okay with not hearing the Pastor call your name or the person you serve acknowledging you in a public way? I mentioned earlier in this book we are in the middle of a global pandemic. The church has had to learn to do ministry a different way. In the beginning the church was still serving. Yet, after three months turned to ten months, the tune changed. People became comfortable sitting on the sidelines and becoming gluttons for the Word, logging on every

Sunday. However, being the church halted. While in the building, members were quick to shout, "we are the church". When the brick and mortar building closed, the desire to serve did also.

As a Pastor, nothing saddens me more than to see the needs of the church family, community, city, and country while those who profess to be children of God sit idly by. What if Peter and John had not persisted in ministry? Would the New Testament church have ceased to exist? Just in case you are wondering, these are the things that keep Pastors up at night. While we are only called to plant the seed of God's Word, it saddens us when we see members of our congregation not bearing any fruit. We see them only doing the bare minimum and that is usually only when asked. Let me go off script for a minute and say, this is why the Pastor needs your prayers. A Pastor who truly has a servant's heart only wants the best for the people God has given them to shepherd. Not a day should go by when you do not pray for your Pastor. Even during a global pandemic, they are praying, preparing, and praying some more to hear from God to feed you the truth of God's Word.

Now back to Acts 4. There was not even a hint of hesitation to continue preaching Jesus. Why? Because the decision was not made by them. It was made by Jesus when He said, **"All authority in heaven and on earth has been given to me. [19] Go therefore and make disciples of all nations, baptizing them in the name of the Father** and of the Son and of the Holy Spirit, [20] teaching them to observe all that I have commanded you. And behold, I am with you always, to the end of the age." (Matthew 28: 18-20)

What a bold statement to make? When they took up their nets to follow Jesus years before, they now understood they were not called by chance. Jesus, who knows all, selected specific individuals knowing what the rest of their lives would look like. He knew what He had placed inside of them. **(Eph. 2:10)** Peter and John knew this was not the time to go back fishing, but instead to stand in the power of God. Remember both Peter and John had seen Jesus not only perform miracles, they saw Him never waiver in His commitment to His Father. John, standing at the foot of the cross, and witnessed Him laying down His life. They saw how diligent He was in communing with His Father. They saw He made no decision without prayer. And this is what the people witnessed. They had experienced two individuals who placed all their trust in God. How do I know? Because after the sentencing came down, their response was, **"Whether it is right in the sight of God to listen to you rather than to God, you must judge, [20] for we cannot but speak of what we have seen and heard." (Acts 4:19-20)**

Do you see what a true witness produces? It produces others who want to follow. I mentioned that their prayer acknowledged God and recognized His sovereignty. Even more important than that, I must point out that the prayer was on one accord. This means there weren't some praying and others wondering about what to cook for dinner. There weren't some praying for the ministry of Peter and John to continue while others were praying that it be demolished. Their convictions about Christ caused them to combine their efforts and go before God with one mind and one spirit.

It's like in the movie, Drumline, starring Nick Cannon. Nick played Mr. Devin Miles, aka Minnie Me. Devin was a bit of a hothead. He had talent and wanted to make sure everyone knew it. In a pivotal scene, Sean played by Leonard Roberts, is in the band room to lay down some tracks. An argument takes place where Devin repeats over and over again, "Say I'm better than you." Sean concedes and says what I consider to be the point I want to stress. He said, "You're the best, Devon! But when we're on the field, nobody hears you! They hear the band."

In a band there are many different instruments and within each section there are many different parts. There is first clarinet and second clarinet. There is the snare drum and the base drum. If any of the band members decided to showboat and input their own solo or play something not on the sheet music, the result of a beautiful, melodic piece would not be heard. It is not the fact that God would honor a prayer given against someone. I want you to understand the power of unified prayer.

Some wonder why the church of today is not that powerful. Is it because God has changed? Absolutely not! It is because the church has forgotten we all serve the same God and when one church glorifies God, we all do. This is not a competition. One band. One sound. One mind. One spirit. Do you have any idea what the church universal would be able to accomplish for God if we were on one accord? Can you imagine the lives that would be saved and how much God's kingdom would expand? The thought of it blows my mind. I still believe in the church. I still believe there are great things for us to accomplish in the name of Jesus. Do you not know, there is power in the name of Jesus? That is not just a Tasha Cobbs-Leonard song. That is a verse from the inspired Word of God. **Philippians 2:9-11** says, **[9] Therefore God has highly exalted him and bestowed on him the name that is above every name, [10] so that at the name of Jesus every knee should bow, in heaven and on earth and under the earth, [11] and every tongue confess that Jesus Christ is Lord, to the glory of God the Father.**

There is no power in Buddha, Muhammad, any dictator, president or king. All will have to bow to the name of Jesus. Status and stature carry no weight. Even Jesus grew. **Luke 2:52** says, **And Jesus increased in wisdom and in stature and in favor with God and man.** There is no such thing as a solo witness. Paul said, when there were grumblings in the church at Corinth, **"I planted, Apollos** watered, but God gave the growth." (1 Corinthians 3:6) There are many verses in the Bible addressing the importance of praying on one accord.

> **"Again I say unto you, That if two of you shall <u>agree</u> on earth as touching anything that they shall ask, it shall be done for them of my Father which is in heaven" (Matthew 18:19).**

> **"Therefore I say unto you, What things soever ye desire, when ye pray, <u>believe</u> that ye receive them, and ye shall have them" (Mark 11:24).**

> **"Confess your faults one to another, and pray one for another, that ye may be healed. The effectual <u>fervent</u> prayer of a righteous man availeth much" (James 5:16)**

> **"And ye shall seek me, and find me, when ye shall search for me with all your heart" (Jeremiah 29:13).**

I must point out the individuals praying had conviction because the providence of God had already been proven in the words David spoke and the death of Christ. **(v. 25)** In **Psalm 2:1-2**, David spoke of the opposition men would face. **"Him, being delivered by the determinate counsel and foreknowledge of God, ye have taken, and by wicked hands have crucified and slain" (Acts 2:23).** These words are evidence to the death, burial and resurrection of Jesus. And still today people stand in opposition to the church. The good news is their opposition is to no avail. It is a waste of time because there is no one greater than God. And we have no reason to fear because that power resides inside us through the Holy Spirit. What a world this would be if the church stood mightily in the power of God! Remember what John wrote in **1 John 4:4.** Because greater is He that is within you, than He that is in the world. He wasn't telling us what he had heard. John was telling us what he had experienced.

What frightens you as a child of God? What is it that hinders you from telling others about Jesus wherever you go? What would it take for you not to run at the first sign of trouble? What if Jesus stopped His journey to the cross after the first lash? The answer is prayer. Our prayers must be faith-filled, focused and fervent. We must ask God to be fearless in the face of opposition. We must ask God for, what the old church used to say, holy boldness. This was a reminder that everything they were doing was empowered by God. He was doing the speaking. He was doing the healing. He was doing the saving. And furthermore, **What then shall we say to these things? If God is for us, who can be against us? (Romans 8:31)**

Just in case you are still teetering between two opinions, I want to conclude this day by talking about the results of the prayer. We dealt with the requests, now let's deal with the results. Upon conclusion of the prayer Mark said, the place in which they were gathered together was shaken. **(v.31)** This was an indication of the physical power of God. God was speaking through His creation. The next thing that happened was they were all filled with the Holy Spirit **(v.31)** This was a refreshing of the Holy Spirit. They needed the Holy Spirit to continue in the work. **"But ye shall receive power, after that the Holy Ghost is come upon you: and ye shall be witnesses unto me both in Jerusalem, and in all Judaea, and in Samaria, and unto the uttermost part of the earth" (Acts 1:8).** Sometimes God has to give us a little extra to perform what is required of us. Lastly, we see that God answered their prayer. They continued to speak boldly about Jesus.

"And he spake boldly in the name of the Lord Jesus, and disputed against the Grecians: but they went about to slay him" (Acts 9:29).

"Long time therefore abode they speaking boldly in the Lord, which gave testimony unto the word of his grace, and granted signs and wonders to be done by their hands" (Acts 14:3).

"And he went into the synagogue, and spake boldly for the space of three months, disputing and persuading the things concerning the kingdom of God" (Acts 19:8).

"These things speak, and exhort, and rebuke with all authority. Let no man despise thee" (Titus 2:15).

Great things happen when we walk in faith and not fear. Souls are saved when we walk in faith and not fear. Believers are edified when we walk in faith and not fear. Families are healed. Marriages are restored. Genuine love that comes from God is spread. God is glorified in our obedience to walk in faith and not fear. No matter what year you may read this book, the world will still need fearless soldiers in the army of the Lord who declare, **"For if we live, we live to the Lord, and if we die, we die to the Lord. So then, whether we live or whether we die, we are the Lord's." (Romans 14:8).** What will your prayer be? Will you pray for boldness to witness to others wherever you are? Will you pray for God to place people in your path that you might share the Gospel of Jesus Christ? Will you pray and ask God to help you to live for Him without compromise and with a true commitment. Will you sing the old Canton Spirituals song?

"I'll go if I have to go by myself?
If my mother
don't go
my father
don't go
my sister
don't go
or my brother
don't go,
I'll go if have to go by myself.

God did not leave us here to accumulate earthly wealth. We are still here because God has given us another day to live for Him without fear.

"Do not pray for easy lives," wrote Phillips Brooks. "Pray to be stronger men and women. Do not pray for tasks equal to your powers. Pray for powers equal to your tasks."

Will you let that be your prayer today?

9 A PRAYER TO NOT BECOME THE WEAKEST LINK

We who are strong have an obligation to bear with the failings of the weak, and not to please ourselves. ²Let each of us please his neighbor for his good, to build him up. ³For Christ did not please himself, but as it is written, "The reproaches of those who reproached you fell on me." ⁴For whatever was written in former days was written for our instruction, that through endurance and through the encouragement of the Scriptures we might have hope. ⁵May the God of endurance and encouragement grant you to live in such harmony with one another, in accord with Christ Jesus, ⁶that together you may with one voice glorify the God and Father of our Lord Jesus Christ. ⁷Therefore welcome one another as Christ has welcomed you, for the glory of God.
Romans 15:1-7

Pastoring is not for the faint at heart. We have the assignment of standing before the broken, bent and bothered. We have to stand week after week in front of people who are sick, stagnant, and stubborn. The church is full of those who have been misused, mishandled, and mistreated. The congregation is comprised of those with family, financial, and forgiveness issues. Pastors must stand and preach with their own marital, ministry, and message problems. We stand in front of people who God has brought together and yet they don't get along. We know the answer is in the Word of God. And yet, we see members of our congregation outright tell God no to the message that has been preached.

The Pastor has to live out John 15 daily in order to do his or her assignment in a manner that pleases God. **⁴Abide in me, and I in you. As the branch cannot bear fruit by itself, unless it abides in the vine, neither can you, unless you abide in me. ⁵I am the vine; you are the branches. Whoever abides in me and I in him, he it is that bears much fruit, for apart from me you can do nothing. John 15:4-6** One of the most difficult assignments for Pastors is helping people to understand their common bond through the blood of Jesus. Not only is fellowship with the Father important. Fellowship with the saints is also important. One of the key verses we have to keep at the forefront of our minds is **1 John 4:8. Anyone who does not love does not know God because God is love.** Drop down to **1 John 4:20-21** where we find these words. **If anyone says, "I love God," and hates his brother, he is a liar; for he who does not love his brother whom he has seen cannot love God whom he has not seen. ²¹ And this commandment we have from him: whoever loves God must also love his brother.**

I told you all this to prepare the ground for the planting of today's focus Scripture. It is inevitable Christians are going to disagree. If we trace the steps of the Old Testament we see family feuds, fights for power and prestige, fights between the rich and poor. In the New Testament the dynamic changes because now we see fights between the Jews and the Gentiles. The Jews were raised in a really legalistic background while the Gentiles never had to worry about any of those things. One group believed it was a sin to eat meat so they ate only vegetables. Another group did not get down with holy days. It would have been good if they would have kept their beliefs in their respective groups but they did not.

If you are having a hard time painting a mental picture of what this looks like. Picture the mothers of the church versus the young adults of the church. Picture someone who grew up in church versus someone who is not aware you stand when the Word of God is being read and you don't walk during invitation. Think about the new member who is led by the Holy Spirit to join your church and is treated as an outcast when they try to serve. It would also be equivalent to some who put levels on sin and those who understand the real intent of the second commandment.

Let me say this. Not all Christians are going to think the same. This has been evident in 2020 with the discord between white evangelicals and people of color. It has always been apparent in the various religions. Paul wanted the church of Rome to understand disunity is okay; however, unity must be when it comes to the Word of God. For example, true Christians not only must believe in God, they must also believe in the incarnate Jesus. They must believe that He was born, died, was buried, and rose again on the third day. This is an essential doctrine. Whether or not women can wear pants is nonessential. Whether or not we wear white every fifth Sunday is nonessential. This brings to mind the German Lutheran theologian of the early seventeenth century, Rupertus Meldenius who coined the phrase, "In essentials unity, in non-essentials liberty, in all things love."

Paul wanted the church to understand that in the same way we were received by God, we are to receive others. God did not require us to be clean before salvation. He accepted our acknowledgement of being lost and enrolled us in the school of faith to become more like Him. There is no greater failure of the church than for someone to come in and feel unwanted. God is inclusive and His children should be also. To insert our personal prejudices and beliefs into the body of Christ is wrong. I pray often for those who are saved to take a moment to go back to the time when they were lost and Jesus found them. I believe God's heart is broken every time He sees His children argue over things that do not matter to Him. I am the first Pastor to say when I am teaching, "If God did not say it, my place is not to make something up by speaking my own personal beliefs." All Christians should live by this.

In the school of faith there are those who are mature and those who are immature. Maturity has nothing to do with age or time on the church roll. Maturity has to do with how much of your life is lived out loud for Christ. Truth be told, all of us should always be growing and it takes other believers to help us along. Timothy had Paul. Ruth had Naomi. Eunice had Lois. Those who are new to the faith need someone to help them understand that God has not deserted them when they fall. Those who have been forgiven after being saved need someone to help them understand God will still forgive them. **(1 John 1:9)**. Those who are mature need to pray for instead of condemning those who make mistakes. Let them know shame comes from the devil. The Bible says.

But the Lord GOD helps me; therefore I have not been disgraced; therefore I have set my face like a flint, and I know that I shall not be put to shame. Isaiah 50:7

I sought the LORD, and he answered me and delivered me from all my fears. Those who look to him are radiant, and their faces shall never be ashamed. Psalm 34:4-5

And now, little children, abide in him, so that when he appears we may have confidence and not shrink from him in shame at his coming. 1 John 2:28

The mature are placed in the body of Christ to build others up. Mature believers are to serve as restorers. Mature believers are to be trusted confidantes of our baby Christians. Mature believers are in churches to shut down gossip. Mature believers are in churches to serve as examples. Their responsibility is to respond to situations within the body of Christ with what the Word of God says. Mature believers are accepting, acknowledging, and agreeable. When a new member joins the church, they move from their regular seat and sit next to them. When there is a dinner in the fellowship hall, they forego their regular seat to go sit and welcome the new sheep to the fold. These may seem like miniscule things. I assure you they are not.

Weak believers are described in Romans 14. They are those who despise, judge, condemns, murmurs, gossips, and criticizes. A weak Christian is the one who is opinionated but not indoctrinated in the Word of God. Tradition is more relevant than true biblical teaching. Things must be done their way for them to support it. They have tenure without transformation. Their conversation is sounding brass and tinkling cymbals.

The church of today has lost the true meaning of **Romans 12:2. Do not be conformed to this world, but be transformed by the renewal of your mind, that by testing you may discern what is the will of God, what is good and acceptable and perfect.** The drawing instrument of the church has changed from the Word of God to flashing lights and playtime for children. This is not a statement to condemn the churches that have these things. It is just to say, too often these things take the spotlight from our Lord and Savior Jesus Christ. Church is being taught in some places the same way the serpent approached Eve. "Did God actually say that?" **(Genesis 3:1)** Excuses are made for sinful behaviors. Pastors are condemned who continue to preach on sin. When they Bible clearly says, **"How then will they call on him in whom they have not believed? And how are they to believe in him of whom they have not heard? And how are they to hear without someone preaching?" Romans 10:14**

An important principle Paul is attempting to get across is true love that comes from God, and not selfishness. Let's look to Jesus for our example.

"For God so loved the world, that he gave his only Son, that whoever believes in him should not perish but have eternal life. John 3:16

But God shows his love for us in that while we were still sinners, Christ died for us. Romans 5:8

For you know the grace of our Lord Jesus Christ, that though he was rich, yet for your sake he became poor, so that you by his poverty might become rich. 2 Corinthians 8:9

[5] Have this mind among yourselves, which is yours in Christ Jesus, [6] who, though he was in the form of God, did not count equality with God a thing to be grasped, [7] but emptied himself, by taking the form of a servant, being born in the likeness of men. [8] And being found in human form, he humbled himself by becoming obedient to the point of death, even death on a cross. Philippians 2:5-8

One of the reasons mental illness goes untreated is those who are diagnosed do not want to be a burden to those around them. They try to express themselves when in truth, they really don't know or understand what they are feeling. After faking it for so long the mask comes off and they crash. Why did I tell you this? Because we know the church is made up of strong and weak Christians, there are weak Christians who do not lean on the help of other strong believers because they feel they are a burden. They feel they will be judged for their failures. God expects the strong to encourage the weak not simply endure them. Do you think Jesus felt like going without food to spread the gospel? Do you think He was smiling while being beaten before being hung on the cross? The answer is found in His prayer in the Garden of Gethsemane.

Sacrifice is a sign of a mature Christian. Mature Christians sacrifice their feelings for the fallen. Mature Christians faces their demons to help the drifting. Mature Christians give up their rights for the rejected. Are you getting the picture? Being a Christian is about living out loud. It is not about how much you wave your hands or say amen. It is not about how often you dawn the doors of the church building. Being a Christian is about allowing someone to see your growth process. It is privately pulling someone aside when you see them going down a path you went down and God delivered you and being their support system. Mature Christians help others grow.

How do we get to the place of unselfishness? Paul says we get our power from the Word of God and prayer. Are you surprised? We must confess we don't know everything and seek the answers in the Word of God. Then we must follow-up in prayer asking God to help us to see ourselves in the passage of Scripture we read. Many Christians feel they are alone. They attend church every Sunday. They wait for that mature believer to reach out to them and offer a hand or shoulder to lean on. They wait and they wait, and no one comes. So, they miss one Sunday and then two or three until they are eventually at home.

Paul tells us we are to bear with the weak. This does not mean we put up with their wrong. It means we remember how patient God is with us and so we support and carry the weak until they are strong enough to stand on their own. There is an organization in the world who understands this concept. The organization is Alcohols Anonymous. After you admit you are an alcoholic, you get a sponsor. The sponsor is there to help the alcoholic when they are tempted to take a drink. They are there to listen when the person is feeling weak.

Strong Christians must be aware of how they are a stumbling block when they are more legalistic than loving. One unkind word may destroy someone's character. In **1 Corinthians 8-9** we find an issue of eating meat that has been offered up to idols in heathen temples. His answer was that knowledge and love must work together. Strong Christians may know what the Bible says. What they must learn how to do is ask God for the way to communicate it to their brother or sister.

The Sunday School teacher may have a glass of wine. Should he or she invite the class over for wine and cheese night? Probably not. The Sunday School teacher must live in such a way that pauses and thinks, "How will this affect my brother or sister?" The teacher may not know one of the students is a recovering alcoholic. A group of men who have been married for a long time may sit around discussing their wives. It is not the most pleasant conversation. A newly married man has been invited. He has already had his first argument with his new bride. Should the conversation stay the same? Probably not. This group of sage men should take a moment to encourage the young man and not to fill his head with negativity. Am I making sense?

And he said to his disciples, "Temptations to sin are sure to come, but woe to the one through whom they come! It would be better for him if a millstone were hung around his neck and he were cast into the sea than that he should cause one of these little ones to sin. Luke 17:1-2

Therefore let us not pass judgment on one another any longer, but rather decide never to put a stumbling block or hindrance in the way of a brother. Romans 14:13

[15] Do your best to present yourself to God as one approved, a worker who has no need to be ashamed, rightly handling the word of truth. [16] But avoid irreverent babble, for it will lead people into more and more ungodliness, [17] and their talk will spread like gangrene. 2 Timothy 2:15-16

Whoever loves his brother abides in the light, and in him there is no cause for stumbling. 1 John 2:10

The body of Christ should have a goal of unity. Unity glorifies God. We are all individuals created in the image of God. We are unified by a person, Jesus Christ. We are united in purpose. Our purpose is evangelism. We are united through a promise. **John 14:1-3** tells us,

"Let not your hearts be troubled. Believe in God; believe also in me. ² In my Father's house are many rooms. If it were not so, would I have told you that I go to prepare a place for you? ³ And if I go and prepare a place for you, I will come again and will take you to myself, that where I am you may be also. Because of these three things that bind us together, we should be able to work together. We are not the same. Even identical twins have differences. Siblings who come from the same parents are different. But when a DNA test is performed they are proven to be one family.

Paul did not say we are to be the same. Paul said we are to be one. Remember Jesus' prayer. He prayed His disciples were one as He and the Father are one. We are one body with many members.

¹² For just as the body is one and has many members, and all the members of the body, though many, are one body, so it is with Christ. ¹³ For in one Spirit we were all baptized into one body— Jews or Greeks, slavesˡ or free—and all were made to drink of one Spirit.

¹⁴ For the body does not consist of one member but of many. ¹⁵ If the foot should say, "Because I am not a hand, I do not belong to the body," that would not make it any less a part of the body. ¹⁶ And if the ear should say, "Because I am not an eye, I do not belong to the body," that would not make it any less a part of the body. ¹⁷ If the whole body were an eye, where would be the sense of hearing? If the whole body were an ear, where

would be the sense of smell? [18] But as it is, God arranged the members in the body, each one of them, as he chose. [19] If all were a single member, where would the body be? [20] As it is, there are many parts, yet one body.

[21] The eye cannot say to the hand, "I have no need of you," nor again the head to the feet, "I have no need of you." [22] On the contrary, the parts of the body that seem to be weaker are indispensable, [23] and on those parts of the body that we think less honorable we bestow the greater honor, and our unpresentable parts are treated with greater modesty, [24] which our more presentable parts do not require. But God has so composed the body, giving greater honor to the part that lacked it, [25] that there may be no division in the body, but that the members may have the same care for one another. [26] If one member suffers, all suffer together; if one member is honored, all rejoice together. 1 Corinthians 12:12-26

We must be intentional about it. We must work to live and serve in harmony. The word we speak as we minister must not vary from person to person. Grace and mercy must be extended to others universally. These things make up a strong church. No one is too bad to be received by Christ. Therefore, no one should be considered too bad for us to receive them. From the back door to the front door, every member should be treated with kindness and compassion. No one is too sinful. No one should be rejected. Everyone should be accepted. Again, we look to the Word of God.

"Now when the apostles which were at Jerusalem heard that Samaria [a despised people] had received the word of God, they sent unto them Peter and John" Acts 8:14

"That ye may with one mind and one mouth glorify God, even the Father of our Lord Jesus Christ" Romans 15:6

"There is neither Jew nor Greek, there is neither bond nor free, there is neither male nor female: for ye are all one in Christ Jesus" Galatians 3:28

Remember this. The standard of unity for the body of Christ is no less than God the Father, God the Son, and God the Holy Spirit. This unity is not superficial smiles and fake hugs. It goes beyond phony Sunday morning relationships and tolerance of one another in ministry outreach. This unity reaches above titles and positions in the church and separate ministry groups. It abides in a group of people who have had their bad reputations cleared by the blood of Jesus. Their sins have been cast into the sea of forgetfulness. The people who are a part of this unity have made a commitment to God not to be the weakest link. There is a sincere love for other believers. There is authentic fellowship. There is genuine mentorship. There is a welcome sign that reaches past the front door and extends to the heart of every person who is a member of the congregation. The strong consider it an honor to encourage and support the weak. Selfishness has been replaced with selflessness. The church has become the house Jesus built. God is proud and the church continues to grow. True ministry goes forth. The then weak become strong and begin to shoulder the burdens of the now weak. And the church is blessed.

**Behold, how good and pleasant it is
when brothers dwell in unity!
² It is like the precious oil on the head,
running down on the beard,
on the beard of Aaron,
running down on the collar of his robes!
³ It is like the dew of Hermon,
which falls on the mountains of Zion!
For there the LORD has commanded the blessing,
life forevermore.
Psalm 133:1-3**

"

10 A PRAYER REQUESTING PROPER WEAPONS FOR PERSISTENT WARFARE

³ For though we walk in the flesh, we are not waging war according to the flesh. ⁴ For the weapons of our warfare are not of the flesh but have divine power to destroy strongholds. ⁵ We destroy arguments and every lofty opinion raised against the knowledge of God, and take every thought captive to obey Christ, ⁶ being ready to punish every disobedience, when your obedience is complete. 2 Corinthians 10:3-6

There are eight primary reasons for war. They are economic gain, territorial gain, religion, nationalism, revenge, civil war, revolutionary war, and defensive war. In the art of war, it is imperative that you, not only, know the reason to fight; you must also know who the right foe is. While this is rather easy to do in the earthly realm, it is difficult for Christians to do in the spiritual realm while living here on earth.

Why is this so difficult for Christians to comprehend? I contend it is because we must have someone to blame and it is easier to blame someone we can see rather than someone who is invisible. A person's natural defense mechanism is to strike back when under attack. We are taught to strike back with our words and/or our actions. We understand we were born into a dark, dismal and depraved world. What we tend to forget is we all still walk in the flesh.

Salvation does not exempt us from evil. Evil is inevitable. In fact, we have it much easier before salvation because the enemy has no reason to bother those who are already his. When Paul speaks to us of spiritual warfare, it is not a myth. When we became friends with God, we became an enemy of Satan. Therefore, we do wrestle daily against **'the rulers, against the authorities, against the cosmic powers over this present darkness, against the spiritual forces of evil in the heavenly places. (Ephesians 6:12)**

Once we understand we do not war (fight) according to the flesh, we can move on to understanding the weaponry God has given us. As in war, we must have a strategy. Our strategy must come from the Divine, our Commander-in-Chief. Without Him leading and guiding us, we will not win. So, what are the weapons Paul is referring to in verse four? He is referring to the weapons found in Ephesians 6.

Pause and read **Ephesians 6:14-18. Stand therefore, having fastened on the belt of truth, and having put on the breastplate of righteousness, [15]and, as shoes for your feet, having put on the readiness given by the gospel of peace. [16]In all circumstances take up the shield of faith, with which you can extinguish all the flaming darts of the evil one; [17]and take the helmet of salvation, and the sword of the Spirit, which is the word of God, [18]praying at all times in the Spirit, with all prayer and supplication.**

According to these verses there are seven weapons we need when engaged in spiritual warfare. We need the belt of truth to fight against the father of lies. We need the breastplate of righteousness to remember the imputed righteousness we received and also the righteousness we must walk in every day. We need to have our feet shod with peace. This means our presence should bring peace with it to defuse negative situations. We need the shield of faith that is portable and able to defend us no matter where the attack is coming from. We need the helmet of salvation so when we, not if, we mess up we are confident of the fact we are still saved. We need to sword of the Spirit because there is only one thing that will win against darkness and that is light. It is the Word of God that is a lamp and light. And then we must pray anywhere, anytime and for anything which gives us a straight shot to our Commander.

When we fail to arm ourselves with the divine weapons God has given us, we fight absent of God's divine power. This means no matter what we do in the battle we will not be victorious. Only God can demolish those things that have been fortified in our minds and hearts. Only God can destroy those thoughts that have been instilled in us since childhood. Only God can dismantle the very barrier you have put up that keeps you from serving Him with your whole heart.

This is nothing for us to play with. The greater your assignment, the greater the attack. You cannot afford to play patty cake with the devil. You cannot afford to struggle in your own strength. The enemy does not fight fair and we live in a world that belongs to Him and doesn't fight fair either. The Bible tells us the thief comes to steal, kill and destroy. **(John 10:10)** And believe me when I tell you, he never stops. Just when you think he has left you alone and become comfortable, here he comes. What did he say when God asked him **"From where had he come?"** His response was, **"From going to and fro on the earth, and from walking up and down on it." (Job 1:7)** 1 **Peter** 5:8 says, **Be sober-minded; be watchful.**

Your adversary the devil prowls around like a roaring lion, seeking someone to devour. Do you think God placed these verses in the Bible for no reason? Of course not! He wanted us to always be on guard against the enemy. He wanted to dispel the myth the enemy is some mystical being.

Just think about it. When we learn not to wage war according to the flesh the stronghold is destroyed. When we learn not to wage war according to the flesh, and we begin to ignore the immaterial and focus on the material, the plan of the enemy is penetrated and then demolished. The key to destroying the lies from the enemy is discipline. We must be as dedicated to putting on the whole armor of God as we are clothing ourselves. We must be as dedicated to putting on the whole armor of God as we are eating. It is that serious.

We live in a world where false teaching runs rampant. Anyone with a smart phone can call himself or herself a preacher and gain a following. Truth has become the new hate speech. People do not want to hear about their responsibilities as Christians. They only want to hear what God will do for them. Individuals who have been in church all their lives are spreading the false doctrine. There is no longer a belief we should "study to show thyself approved unto God". The popular thing of today is to be spoon-fed. And preacher, be careful not to talk too much about those things that will challenge me because you know with church being online, I can just tune you out and go to someone else's broadcast.

We live in a world today where people do not want to sit in silence. The spiritual discipline of prayer has become one-sided. God let me tell you what I need, in Jesus' name amen. We may tune into the virtual worship service, but we do not take any notes or pause and ask God what He wanted us to see that would continue to change us into the image of His Son. It is easier to dislike someone because we don't really love ourselves. It is easier to react rather than respond. We have stopped letting the words of our mouth and the meditation of our hearts be acceptable in God's sight. We spend more time feeding our negative thoughts than we do in the Word of God. And our lives are suffering.

As Christians we have a habit of saying we want everything God has for us, but do we really? To receive everything God has for us we must be obedient to His Word. **All Scripture is breathed out by God and profitable for teaching, for reproof, for correction, and for training in righteousness, that the man of God may be complete, equipped for every good work. (2 Timothy 3:16-17)**. It is our obedience that shows God we love Him. This is precisely why we must take every thought captive. **(v.5)** Our thoughts must be controlled and subjected unto Christ.

Those random thoughts we have that no one knows about must be surrendered to Christ. Our impulsive actions must be surrendered to Christ. Those barriers we have erected against the truth of God's Word must be surrendered to Christ. Before the thought leaves our lips, we must surrender it to Christ and see if He gives it permission to be spoken. Before that reaction is put into motion, it must be surrendered. And I know some of you reading this will think, that is too much. That is just who I am. I can say what I want and ask for forgiveness later. I can react how I want and change later. I need the satisfaction of instant retaliation. If you are thinking this after reading the first part of today's devotion, start today over. Pray and then begin reading again.

The main idea of today is to help you to understand, carnal weapons will not conquer the enemy. In all things we are more than conquerors, but that is only **"through Him that loved us." (Romans 8:37).** You cannot expect to be more than a conqueror doing things the world's way. Let me ask you a question. What did you think Jesus meant when He said, **"If anyone would come after me, let him deny himself and take up his cross daily and follow me?" (Luke 9:23)** Too many times we have the attitude of the scribe or the disciple who came to Jesus in **Matthew 8.** Jesus let the scribe know there was a rough journey ahead. It was a journey where, **"Foxes have holes, and birds of the air have nests, but the Son of Man has nowhere to lay**

his head." (Matthew 8:20) And to the disciple who wanted to go and bury his father, Jesus replied, **"Follow me, and leave the dead to bury their own dead." (Matthew 8:21).** It was at this point Jesus was letting them know there is nothing and no one more important doing what He called them to do.

I know this may appear to be harsh for some who are comfortably living your lives the way you always have. I am referring to those who do what you want, say what you want, and go where you want. The furthest thought from your mind is truly being obedient to God. Your life is pretty good as is. Why do you need to change anything? Hence, the reason Paul had to write this. Your life reflects more of your independence than your dependence on Christ. Paul wrote this because the Judaizers of that day accused him of being timid and weak when in the presence of the people. Paul did this because he wanted only to exalt the Savior. He wanted his life to represent Jesus by walking and talking in the way Jesus walked. He had left that life of antagonism and persecution to now sit down and instead stand up for Jesus. If he had responded the way they wanted him to respond he would be teaching them to fight in the flesh. That was not his assignment. His assignment was to build up the church of Jesus Christ, not the church of Paul.

The problem Paul was facing is much like the world today. Paul was being judged by the outward appearance of his ministry than by the fruit being produced. You know, like a church being considered successful based on the size and the number of people in the membership. The Judaizers wanted to be a part of a church where Paul was popular. They did not care about souls being saved or the number of baptisms. They wanted Paul to exalt himself and that would give them status. They did not understand those were fleshly measuring points and not spiritual ones.

In America we just finished a presidential election. Before the voting took place both candidates ran a campaign. The purpose of the campaign was to convince the citizens of the United States to vote for him. There were times when the campaign became very ugly. One of the candidates tried to discredit the other with a smear campaign. This is when the candidate digs up the most damaging things from the opponent's past. Why am I telling you this? Because the word warfare literally means campaign. Paul wanted us to know the enemy has launched a campaign to discredit the presence, promises and power of our God. There is nothing he will not do. He works tirelessly to manipulate your mind, chisel away your character, and misrepresent the message from above. He is depending on you not to search the Scriptures for yourself. He wants you to become so wrapped up in the things of the world that spiritual things are optional.

His instructions here in 2 Corinthians 10 are to ensure you do not become a victim of his scheme and instead be victorious through the strength of the Lord. Paul wanted to let us know our efforts would be unsuccessful if we try to play a tit for tat game with the devil. It would be impossible to beat the enemy at something he has worked so hard to perfect. He eats, sleeps, and breathes deception. He has been fighting a losing battle against Jesus for a very long time. And yet, he does not give up. He doesn't give up because he is waiting for some poor, misguided soul to undervalue the whole armor of God. He is waiting for some delusional saint to believe he or she has made it this far on their own. He is waiting for the one person who will allow one test to stop him or her from trusting. He wants to find the one person who will let failure dry up his or her faith. That is how the enemy gets in. He waits for us to try it God's way and when it doesn't work out the way we thought it should. We fall back into our old ways.

Paul wants us to use spiritual weapons alone to fight Satan. He encourages us to continue in prayer, the Word of God, love, and let the power of the Holy Spirit work in our lives. Personality, performance and your position will only take you so far. They may appear to take you far in the world; however, these are the exact things that will stifle your spiritual growth. We must never forget that in Christ we are new creatures. We must work to lay down the principles of the world and pick up the promises of God. Remembering to look unto Jesus who is the author and finisher of our faith.

I know using spiritual weapons to fight what appears to be a carnal war may appear to be ridiculous to some. I am sure when Joshua and the children of Israel began to march around the walls of Jericho, their opponents thought for sure they would see victory. I am sure when Daniel refused to obey the edict of King Nebuchadnezzar, his loyal subjects who set the trap thought they had won. I bet the bystanders could not wait for the three Hebrew boys to burn up in the fiery furnace so they would incite fear in the rest of the foreigners. However, what all the naysayers and bystanders failed to realize is they were not worried about what they thought. This is why the walls came tumbling down, the mouths of the lions were shut, and the three Hebrew boys did not burn up or have the smell of smoke in their clothes. In all of these situations, those involved desired to make God's name great and so they moved forward in obedience to Him.

The next time someone sees you being mistreated will you pause and plan how to get that person back or will they see you still being kind? When you receive a phone call from an angry friend or relative about what someone has done to him or her, will you remind your friend of what the Word of God says or say you are on your way to get revenge? The next time someone wants to sabotage the work in the church by not participating because they don't like the person over it, will you get people to join your scheme or serve alongside the individual?

We have a responsibility to the saved and the unsaved to always represent Christ. Our lives are to represent Him in all we do. Stop focusing on material success and social prestige. We must learn to keep our lustful appetites in check. The time is now to allow God to control our passions. Our war against the flesh never stops. Your eloquent speech will not win you the victory. Your unmatched intellect will not win you the victory. Your charm and your good looks will not win you the victory. The only thing that will win you the victory is to be ready for the battle. How do you prepare for the battle? **Finally, be strong in the Lord and in the strength of his might. ¹¹Put on the whole armor of God, that you may be able to stand against the schemes of the devil. (Ephesians 6:10-11) Finally, brothers, whatever is true, whatever is honorable, whatever is just, whatever is pure, whatever is lovely, whatever is commendable, if there is any excellence, if there is anything worthy of praise, think about these things. (Philippians 4:8)**

Don't be guilty of exalting your thoughts over godly wisdom and knowledge. **For the Lord gives wisdom; From His mouth come knowledge and understanding. (Proverbs 2:6) But if any of you lacks wisdom, let him ask of God, who gives to all generously and without reproach, and it will be given to him. (James 1:5).** The enemy wants to ruin your relationship with the Father. He wants nothing more than for you and me to doubt the person of God, His love and His goodness. Our prayer must always be for God to remind us of the necessity of the whole armor of God. We must ask God to help us never forget the value of the Word of God. Our lives must reflect the wisdom from God. This is how we remain victorious.

11 A PRAYER OF CONTENTMENT

I must go on boasting. Though there is nothing to be gained by it, I will go on to visions and revelations of the Lord. ²I know a man in Christ who fourteen years ago was caught up to the third heaven—whether in the body or out of the body I do not know, God knows. ³And I know that this man was caught up into paradise—whether in the body or out of the body I do not know, God knows— ⁴and he heard things that cannot be told, which man may not utter. ⁵On behalf of this man I will boast, but on my own behalf I will not boast, except of my weaknesses— ⁶though if I should wish to boast, I would not be a fool, for I would be speaking the truth; but I refrain from it, so that no one may think more of me than he sees in me or hears from me. ⁷So to keep me from becoming conceited because of the surpassing greatness of the revelations, a thorn was given me in the flesh, a messenger of Satan to harass me, to keep me from becoming conceited. ⁸Three times I pleaded with the Lord about this, that it should leave me. ⁹But he said to me, "My grace is sufficient for you, for my power is made perfect in weakness." Therefore I will boast all the more gladly of my weaknesses, so that the power of Christ may rest upon me. ¹⁰For the sake of Christ, then, I am content with weaknesses, insults, hardships, persecutions, and calamities. For when I am weak, then I am strong.

2 Corinthians 12:1-10

What is grace? I am sure you will answer unmerited favor. But what does that really mean? Let's break down the two words and see if that helps you to understand grace. Unmerited, according to Webster's Dictionary, means not adequately earned or deserved. Here are a few examples for you to contemplate. If you have a job and are scheduled to work an eight-hour shift and yet you call in sick. You don't have any paid time off stored up and no vacation time to use. You know you must have a full paycheck in order to meet your financial obligations this week. Friday rolls around and you pick up your check. You open it up hesitantly only to discover you were paid for the eight hours you missed. You did not perform any work duties and yet you were paid. The pay received was unmerited.

Perhaps that illustration did not resonate with you. Let me try another one. Soldiers who serve in the military receive awards for service in combat. You enlist in the military with full expectation one day you will be in combat, boots on the ground. Right before your unit was called to active duty, you become disabled. You cannot fight with the other soldiers who have become your family. You feel worthless and defeated. When your platoon returns from active duty an award ceremony is held to honor the soldiers who risked their lives. You attend to show your support. You hear all the other soldiers' names called, and suddenly you here your name. You know you were not able to fight. You did nothing to deserve it and yet you receive the award. That is another example of unmerited.

Now we will look at the word favor. Finding favor means gaining approval, acceptance, or special benefits or blessings. Human approval can be gained through faithful and effective service. Joseph enjoyed the favor of Potiphar as he wisely administered Potiphar's estate, though ultimately this recognition came through God's blessing (Genesis 39:4 Genesis 39:21). Ruth found favor in the eyes of the wealthy Boaz because of her kindness to her mother-in-law, Naomi (Ruth 2:2 Ruth 2:10 Ruth 2:13). Although David was badly out of favor with Saul, even the Philistines realized how quickly David could have regained favor through his military skill (1 Sam 29:4). A king's favor brought many benefits to the recipient (Prov 16:15).

Now let me see if I can combine the two words and give you the Pastor G, yet biblical translation of grace. Grace is when God sees your dirty, filthy, worthless, undeserving self and still responds to you in the way that will benefit you the most. He has seen everything you have done, are doing and will do and still allows you to play apart in His salvific efforts. The problem I have observed sitting in the under Shepherd's seat is how many people do not realize they have fallen from grace and must be justified in order to get back in right standing with God.

I know you have lived a pretty decent life. And even if you haven't you are saved now and so God should bless you. Our human mind cannot come close to comprehending the true meaning of grace. We are programmed with the concept when you give you receive. When you work, you receive a wage. When you compete in sports and win, you receive a trophy or a medal. When you participate in a competition, you receive a prize. Grace, however, does not work like that. You can serve forty years in ministry and still not do enough to earn grace. You can preach faithfully for fifty or more years and still not do enough to deserve grace. You can usher, do missionary work, lead the prayer ministry, visit the sick-and-shut-in, feed the homeless every week and still not earn grace.

Grace is the free gift of God. If we had to earn it, we would all have our one-way tickets to hell. When you picture Jesus dying on the cross that is a picture of grace. When you sing the lyrics to the hymn Amazing Grace, you should reflect on your life and see grace. Understanding grace requires us to leave all human reasoning and trust the spiritual insight given through the wisdom and knowledge of God.

One man who understood grace was the Apostle Paul. Paul the one who said **Indeed, I count everything as loss because of the surpassing worth of knowing Christ Jesus my Lord. For his sake I have suffered the loss of all things and count them as rubbish, in order that I may gain Christ. (Philippians 3:8)** Paul who had received the highest education and been promoted in the ranks said none of that matters. Paul understood he deserved the very punishment he had inflicted on the Christians of the New Testament church. And yet one day on the Damascus Road God extended to him grace. That is when all his problems really began.

When Paul was on the left, he faced critics. And now that he is on the right, the critics appear to be louder. They did not understand why Paul never talked about himself. They did not understand why Paul said the only words that mattered were the ones God told him to speak. **(cf. 1 Corinthians 14:18-19)** This concept sounds foreign to me in the age of social media. Scroll through your personal timelines and weigh the amount of posts from pastors, preachers, biblical teachers, and Christians that give credit to God. When feeding the hungry and clothing the naked, do you hear God's name or their names? When did the decision for a church home depend on the size of the building and the fame of the Pastors more than the souls saved and baptized? When did an association with another human being become more important than an intimate relationship with God? We appear to have this thing backwards. It is no longer if I be lifted up; I'll draw all men unto me. Instead, it is my popularity, prestige, political affiliation, that has gotten me the status I have.

What happened to going after the one? Paul felt this so much that even though he had experienced the dreams and visions they criticized him about, he revealed the story in third person. For fourteen years Paul saw his encounter with God as a special time between him and God only. In this twelfth chapter of 2 Corinthians, he told the story only because God had a more important principle to teach His children. Always remember you owe no one an explanation for your calling. Man has no authority to discredit you. Favor is divinely given at God's discretion. Unfortunately, we spend more time trying to discredit someone's gift than walking in our own. Paul said I will remain silent so that no one will think more of me than I am. (v.6). He did not, however stop exalting the Savior every chance he got.

Paul wanted us to know serving the Lord is not going to be a life free of critics, challenges, and conundrums. It will not be a life free of tests, trials, and trouble. When you are living a life fully devoted to the Lord, all of that is a part of it. It comes with the territory. I tell everyone who serves with me at my church, be prepared for the dislike and even hate, not because you have done anything wrong. It will simply be because of what God has placed on the inside of you. Why do you think God told us not to put a lampshade over our lights? He said it because some of us would be given a light that shines bright wherever we go and even without us turning it on. It is simply God's unmerited favor.

Let me pause for a minute and say, Paul's head knowledge of who he was serving did not stop God from leaving him with a daily reminder that this is not about you, it is about Me. **2 Corinthians 12:7** says, **"So to keep me from becoming conceited *(having a figurative imagination about who I am)* because of the surpassing greatness of the revelations, a thorn was given me in the flesh, a messenger of Satan to harass *(to strike with a clenched fist)* me, to keep me from becoming conceited."** What was the thorn? I do not know, and I will not guess about something God did not bother to tell us. The purpose of the thorn is more important than the picture of the thorn.

God gave Paul the thorn so he would remember to remain humble in everything. He wanted Paul to understand no matter how the people may have praised him, do not get puffed up. Secondly, God wanted Paul to remember, service for the Lord is not an independent venture. Success is dependent upon one's dependence on the Lord. How many times have you experienced or observed someone who is gifted and on fire for the Lord and then there is a change? The change occurs when we forget who gave us the gift. I have been guilty of this very thing. When our building project collapsed, God revealed to me I had begun to believe the hype. This is precisely why I don't put any stake in the praise of people. "Oh Pastor, you sho' did preach today!" "Pastor, that sermon was fire." "Pastor, you preached your face off today." Sure, I appreciate it. However, when I don't see the fruit of

God's Word bearing fruit in the lives of the individuals so full of praise, I am reminded there is still work for me to do.

God does not want us to think we did it on our own. The weaker we are the more God is glorified. This is why attendance at the church does not matter. Your service as a ministry leader does not matter. You can be the most gifted singer and not bring glory to God. You can be the most requested speaker and not bring glory to God. You can put together programs and ministry efforts for the community and God not be glorified. Why is God not glorified? Because your reason for serving is not pure. Your heart is dirty. You're serving with unforgiveness in your heart. Your purpose for serving is personal accolades. If there is one thing 2020 has shown me, serving God, for many, was attached to the building. People may have started out with pure motives, but when people stopped receiving the praises of the people an invisible sign was put up that said; "Closed until in-person worship begins again." This may sound harsh to some. Sorry not sorry. My concern is for your salvation and not your feelings.

What greater testimony to others than for someone to know your background and see you still serving and still praising God. What better way to honor God than by pressing on in the midst of adversity? How many souls will you be able to influence for God when they know you lost everything and yet your generosity never fluctuated. I want to point out two words in verse seven you might have overlooked. Those two words are given me. Most of the time we associate the word given with the word gift. Although the thorn was the source of great affliction for Paul, He considered it a gift from God. When you recognize God is the source of your affliction, you are able to thank Him for it.

Even though Paul was aware of the source of His affliction, He still tried to reason with God three times to remove it. There is a very valuable lesson taught here. Just because God is the source of the affliction does not mean we cannot pray to God about it. Just as Jesus did in the Garden of Gethsemane, Paul prayed three times for God to remove the thorn. And three times God said no. Instead He said to Paul, "I have an inexhaustible supply of grace that is more than enough for every situation you will face." It is ample in amount and fit in character. There is no place you can go where the grace of God cannot find you. There is no season in life when the grace of God cannot reach you. God's grace is sufficient.

I want to take a moment to unteach a principle that has been taught across denominations. This is the principle of God's grace only being equivalent to blessings. Our limited human reasoning sees blessings as material things. In our finite thinking we cannot fathom a job loss being favor. We cannot imagine a divorce is favor. You mean to tell me a loss of a friend can be God's grace? Absolutely! This is why we should never try to force a situation. I know someone who lost their home and persisted in applying for other rental properties receiving a denial each time. In the beginning the denials did not look like favor. In the end, they were favor. They were favor because of the blessing she received in spending unending time with God. One thing, as Christians, we must always remember. **For my thoughts are not your thoughts, neither are my ways your ways, declared the Lord. (Isaiah 55:8)**

There are many types of grace. There is salvific grace. **Ephesians 2:8-9** says, **"For by grace you have been saved through faith. And this is not your own doing; it is the gift of God, not a result of works, so that no one may boast."** There are numerous graces. God does not only give us another chance; He gives us chance after chance after chance. **1 John 1:9** says, **If we confess our sins, he is faithful and just to forgive us our sins and to cleanse us from all unrighteousness.** There is no small print attached to this promise that says, this verse is good up to ten times. I said earlier God's grace is inexhaustible. Paul said, "I really want to do good. I just cannot seem to escape this evil. It follows me everywhere." (Romans 7:21, my emphasis). The good news is wherever evil goes so does the grace of God. The grace of God is the way of escape He promised in 1 Corinthians 10.

Not only is there salvific grace and numerous grace, there is forgiveness grace. I know you think I already talked about forgiveness.

In this case, I am speaking of the grace God gives us to forgive others. No, you cannot forgive others on your own. However, through the grace of God you can. There is no pain you will experience at the hands of others you cannot forgive. You may disobey God and not forgive someone, just know when you do you are out of the will of God. After a while, the unforgiveness you hold on to is a slap in the face to the grace God has given you and thereby unacceptable.

The final grace I want to introduce to you today is new grace. Every morning you rise God is giving you grace to handle the situations and circumstances of today. He knows your spouse is going to make you mad and you just forgave him or her yesterday for the same thing. This is why God gives you new grace in case you try to say you have no more grace for the situation. God knows that child is going to break curfew again. God knows your boss is going to test you by passing you over for that promotion. God know the friend you discussed your idea with is going to post the flyer the night before to make it appear you are copying them. Every single day is an opportunity for us to grow in grace and in the knowledge of our Lord and Savior Jesus Christ. Every day new grace gives us the opportunity to display more of the fruit of the Spirit. **(Galatians 5:22-23)**

Paul concludes this chapter by saying, "I do have a reason to boast." His reason to boast came from those things which would point the people to Christ. An average person may be tempted to give up on this God thing when experiencing weaknesses, insults, hardships, persecutions and calamities. Not Paul. Paul declared I boast in my unforeseen and unwanted circumstances that render me weak. I boast because these are the opportunities when God can really show up in me.

There is nothing I hate more than a toothache. There were times when I would simply take some Tylenol. It never quite did the trick though. I needed a pill packed with a little bit more punch. I needed extra strength Tylenol. This is exactly what the sufficient grace of God is for us. His grace is more than enough to conquer any sickness or disease. It is more than enough to handle your depression and anxiety. His grace is more than enough to handle absolutely anything you will face in this life. The confidence Paul had in the sufficient grace of God allowed him to lift the barriers of fear and anxiety from the situation. This confidence caused him to yield to the sovereign will of God in everything he faced. There was nothing special about Paul. Paul was faced with some of the most dangerous, difficult and deadly situations and he persevered through them.

Our prayer should be to accept the grace given to us by God. Our heart's desire should be to accept the sufficiency of the grace extended even in difficult situations. We must learn to lift the barrier of the finite thoughts we have during hardships and calamities. We must commit to living in the sovereign will of God.

12 A PRAYER TO KEEP IN STEP WITH THE SPIRIT

16 But I say, walk by the Spirit, and you will not gratify the desires of the flesh. 17 For the desires of the flesh are against the Spirit, and the desires of the Spirit are against the flesh, for these are opposed to each other, to keep you from doing the things you want to do. 18 But if you are led by the Spirit, you are not under the law. 19 Now the works of the flesh are evident: sexual immorality, impurity, sensuality, 20 idolatry, sorcery, enmity, strife, jealousy, fits of anger, rivalries, dissensions, divisions, 21 envy,[d] drunkenness, orgies, and things like these. I warn you, as I warned you before, that those who do[e] such things will not inherit the kingdom of God. 22 But the fruit of the Spirit is love, joy, peace, patience, kindness, goodness, faithfulness, 23 gentleness, self-control; against such things there is no law. 24 And those who belong to Christ Jesus have crucified the flesh with its passions and desires. 25 If we live by the Spirit, let us also keep in step with the Spirit. Galatians 5:16-25

I am in awe of swing dancing. I do not know how to do it. I just like watching it. It is amazing how in sync the man and the woman seem to be. They don't miss a beat. I was watching a couple dancing together on social media. I asked my assistant how the woman knows what to do. Her answer was, "The man leads, and you just follow. There are basic steps you learn and once you begin partner dancing it just all comes together. If the woman tries to go her own way or lead, then the dance will get out of step." As I was reading today's text, this analogy helped me to understand what Apostle Paul is trying to tell us. Stay in step with God. Let Him lead.

The Bible says, **Therefore, if anyone is in Christ, he is a new creation. The old has passed away; behold, the new has come. (2 Corinthians 5:17)**. The Bible also tells us that upon conversion our bodies become the temple of the Holy Spirit. **(1 Corinthians 6:19-20)** Although we cannot rid ourselves of the flesh, we can rid ourselves of the lust of the flesh. The flesh is strong. On our own we have no power to fight against it. Read the words of Paul found in **Romans 7:15-20**.

[15] I do not understand what I do. For what I want to do I do not do, but what I hate I do. [16] And if I do what I do not want to do, I agree that the law is good. [17] As it is, it is no longer I myself who do it, but it is sin living in me. [18] For I know that good itself does not dwell in me, that is, in my sinful nature. For I have the

desire to do what is good, but I cannot carry it out. [19] For I do not do the good I want to do, but the evil I do not want to do—this I keep on doing. [20] Now if I do what I do not want to do, it is no longer I who do it, but it is sin living in me that does it.

This is Paul speaking. Paul is the author of over half the New Testament. He was responsible for spreading the gospel to the Gentiles. The fact still remains that as much as Paul desired to do good, he could not. There was a war constantly going on inside him. Remember earlier when I said upon conversion your body becomes the temple of the Holy Spirit. This truth should keep us from becoming puffed up in our victories. For we, like Paul, cannot fight the flesh on our own. It is the Holy Spirit inside us that aides us. The Holy Spirit gives us power in our moments of weakness. The Holy Spirit, you know, the third part of the Holy Trinity. He is able to aid us in times of pressure to do what does not please God. One very important thought I want you to take note of is the flesh and the Holy Spirit cannot peacefully co-exist. The flesh is going to always fight for control. And without the Holy Spirit we will always succumb under the pressure.

Verse 1 of chapter 5 says, **For freedom Christ has set us free; stand firm therefore, and do not submit again to a yoke of slavery.** The Judaizers of Paul's day did not understand grace. They had lived under the law for so long, they felt that grace moved them from law to license. Grace was license to sin. They felt if rules were abolished that surely the church would become unruly. The Judaizers are comparable to the people in church today who still get upset when women wear pants. They are the ones who still believe children should be baptized before they participate in anything at church. They don't want the Pastor to teach about grace because this might change the makeup of the congregation. Pastor, I need you to preach hell, fire and brimstone. This is funny because these individuals don't realize they, too, are the recipients of grace.

What does it mean to live a free life if it does not mean we can do what we want to do and just ask God for forgiveness? Living a free life is for the one who recognizes the sacrifice made by Jesus to free him or her from the law of sin and death. Living a free life is for the one who realizes the extent of the suffering Jesus endured for his or her sake. Living a free life is for the one who regards the Savior as head of his or her life. When one lives a free life, he or she does not do what they want when they want or how they want. We are no longer in bondage; therefore, we must learn how to live a free life.

Before our freedom we were slaves to the flesh. We were slaves to the world and the things of the world. Our flesh was a slave to adultery, fornication, uncleanness, lasciviousness, idolatry, witchcraft, hatred, variance, emulations, wrath, strife, seditions, heresies, envying, murders, drunkenness, and revellings. (**vv. 19-21**)

Whether you committed any of these acts or not, you were a slave to them. You did not have to learn how to do them. They came naturally. When you are engaged in these activities you are not presenting yourself as a living sacrifice, holy and acceptable unto God, which is your spiritual worship. (**Romans 12:1**) When you are engaged in these activities you have put back on the yoke of slavery you have been freed from. I like the show 48 Hours on A&E and the thing that gets me every time is how a person just released commits another crime and winds up right back in jail. I want to yell at the television, "Don't you know you're free!"

The problem differentiating between bondage and freedom is our error in judgment. Too often Christians view their salvation as a life that can no longer be fun. When they read the Bible all they see is what they cannot do. They view life before Christ as living and life after Christ as dead. Have they not read **Ephesians 2:1-6? And you were dead in the trespasses and sins [2] in which you once walked, following the course of this world, following the prince of the power of the air, the spirit that is now at work in the sons of disobedience— [3] among whom we all once lived in the passions of our flesh, carrying out the desires of the body and the mind, and were by nature children of wrath, like the rest of mankind. [4] But God, being rich in mercy, because of the great love with which he loved us, [5] even when we were dead in our**

trespasses, made us alive together with Christ—by grace you have been saved. They place the things of this world at a higher value than eternal life. It hurts my heart when I see and hear this because these individuals are missing out. It is the enemy who comes to steal, kill, and destroy. Jesus came so we would have an abundant life. **(John 10:10)** Do you not know there is nothing you can accomplish in this life that compares to abundant life in Christ?

We all know what it is like to give into the lusts of the flesh. It is usually not someone's personality that draws us to him or her. It is the height, eyes, build, or smile. Then we wait and see if we feel anything and I am not talking about in our hearts. I often tell our young ladies at the church heading to college, it may not be as easy to say no when you have your own place, and someone makes you feel butterflies for the first time. Saints don't have to work to sin. It is our nature. I hear Christians saying all the time we are born in sin and shaped in iniquity. I am beginning to think most of us think of this in the past tense. Yes, we are new creatures; however, there must be a daily decision to live in our newness. Living in the newness of life means we stop trying to fulfill the law and instead walk in the Spirit.

Notice the contrast between the works of the flesh and the fruit of the Spirit. The works of the flesh are performed on the outside while the fruit of the Spirit grow naturally out of our inward change. After we are saved by grace through faith, we begin discipleship lessons. These lessons are taught through the Word of God. As we read the Word of God, we have the necessary steps to live a life yielded to the Holy Spirit. These discipleship lessons develop the roots needed to bear fruit. Understand this child of God, God's desire for us is not just for us to stop doing bad things. His desire is that as we are transformed by the renewing of our minds, we begin to do good things. This is why the law would have never been enough. Think about this. A manufacturing plant is full of machines that work to produce a product. But no matter how much those machines work, they will never be able to grow anything. There is no living aspect to the machine. And something dead can never produce something living. A blender works to produce a fruit smoothie. This same blender, however, could never produce the fruit to make the smoothie. Fruit is living. And good fruit carrying seeds bring about more fruit.

This is why Jesus was born. He was born to die and resurrected to give us life. We would never have been able to do this for one another. Because we were all dead in our trespasses and sins, we would only be able to produce other dead beings. I know some mother reading this is thinking, I have children. I gave them life. Yes, you did give birth, but know this, only Jesus can give life. It is very important for all of us to come to terms with the fact the only good thing about us is the Jesus who lives inside us. This is why it is foolish for the rich to think themselves better than the poor. It is idiotic for white people to think themselves better than people of color. It is unwise for the employed to think themselves better than those who are unemployed. It is apparent anyone who thinks this way is not walking in the Spirit. **For they that are after the flesh do mind the things of the flesh; but they that are after the Spirit the things of the Spirit. Romans 8:5**

Now that we have a pretty good idea of what the works of the flesh are, I want to focus now on the fruit of the Spirit. In 1981, the gospel group The Clark Sisters debuted the song, Walking in the Spirit. The lyrics are as follows.

Moment by moment, day by day
Let me be drunk in your spirit as I constantly pray
Minute, each second, every breath I take
Let me be slain in your spirit morning by morning when I wake

Let me walk in the spirit
Let me move in the spirit
Let me be drunk in the spirit
Let me have the fruit of the spirit

Let me walk in the spirit
Let me move in the spirit
Let me be drunk in the spirit
Let have the fruits of the spirit

Love, joy, peace, long-suffering, gentleness

Goodness, faith, meekness, temperance
If we live in the spirit
Let us walk in the spirit
If we live in the spirit

Also, also, also, also
Let us walk in the spirit

This song was written at a time when gospel music was the Word of God set to music. When we heard songs like these on Sunday morning, they were a reverberation of our Sunday School lessons and Sunday sermons. We would find ourselves humming them as we did our chores. We would hear them played on the record player on Sunday morning. It helped to establish in our minds the importance of walking in the Spirit. We may not have truly understood this concept as children, but the more we grew it became a part of our lives.

God is love and we are to walk in love. (John 3:16) When we walk in God's love, no matter how others act toward us or say about us we don't stop loving them. Isn't this how God loves us? We ignore Him. We lie to Him. We say He has left us. We don't trust Him. We place our hope in man. And yet, He loves us. God gives us joy and we are to walk in joy. **(Romans 5:11)** We have joy, not based on happenings, but based on our knowledge of Jesus. The more we fellowship with Him, the more joy we have. The mere presence of the Holy Spirit should give us joy. This joy can be experienced at all times. People cannot take our joy. Lack of finances should not steal our joy. The absence of an earthly mate should not steal our joy. To have joy is to have Jesus. God also grants us peace and so we are to walk in peace. Remember when Jesus told His disciples, **Peace I leave with you; my peace I give to you. Not as the world gives do, I give to you. Let not your hearts be troubled, neither let them be afraid. John 14:27**

The story is told of a billionaire who asked three different artists to paint their depiction of what peace looks like. The winner would become heir to her fortune. The first artist painted a sailboat in the middle of the ocean with a lone passenger. The sky was blue and the water was calm. He told the billionaire, "This is what I think about when I think of peace. It occurs when I am a million miles away from everything. I am not bothered by my spouse, children, grandchildren or job. It is just me."

The second painter was a young woman in her twenties who painted a beautiful waterfall. The scene was absolutely beautiful. I would imagine the feeling of peace I would experience if I were there. As she was describing her painting, she told the billionaire, "Whenever I cannot sleep I turn on the sound of a waterfall and before I know it I am lulled off to sleep. I close my eyes and imagine myself laying on the rocks in the cool with the sound of the waterfall in my ears.

The final painter was an elderly woman. She had not lived the easiest life. She had been painting for over thirty years and had never made much income from her paintings. She never made a lot of income because she never charged what the paintings were worth. Truth be told, she gave most of them away. The billionaire was quite puzzled by her painting. The painting depicted a very torrential thunderstorm with lightning strikes and upheaval all around. People were running trying to take shelter. Cars were stopped in the middle of the street for lack of visibility to drive any further. When asked how this picture reflected peace the painter replied, "You must look closely my dear. At first glance you see the storm and the chaos. If you look closer, you see a bird perched on a tree branch seemingly undisturbed by the storm. That bird is me. I have learned no matter what is going on around me I can have peace. Peace, for me, is not the lack of chaos but calm in the midst of chaos." The billionaire was amazed and gave the woman her entire fortune.

Ladies and gentlemen, this is the kind of peace God gives to us. It is a peace that surpasses all understanding. **(Philippians 4:6-7)** It is a peace we have when our mind is stayed on Jesus. **(Isaiah 26:3)** It is a peace that is with us always. **(2 Thessalonians 3:16)** It is the peace we receive because of our justification. **(Romans 5:1)** It is a peace for the righteous and not the wicked. **(Isaiah 48:22)** And like all the other God-given fruit, He wants us to share it with others.

Those who are peacemakers will be called the sons of God. **(Matthew 5:9)** God commands us to live peaceably with all. **(Romans 12:18)** We are commanded to let the peace of God rule in our hearts. **(Colossians 3:15)** Another command is for us to strive for peace with everyone. **(Hebrews 12:14)** Do you get the picture? Those who are loved by God should show God's love to others. Those who have God's joy should share it with others. Those who have received God's peace should spread God's peace.

Not only should love, joy and peace be produced in the life of a Christian, out of them should grow long-suffering. William Barclay says if God had been a man, He would have long ago wiped man off the face of the earth because of his terrible disobedience. *(The Letters to the Galatians and Ephesians, p.56)* Here is the hard truth. Christians who bear the fruit of long-suffering never attack. They never strike back. It does not matter the abuse, slander or wrong they encounter from others. How? The Holy Spirit helps them to suffer long through it. Now do you see why walking in the Spirit is so vital for all Christians?

If God were not long-suffering toward us, some of us would not be saved. Let's take a look at some Scripture.

"For my name's sake I defer my anger; for the sake of my praise I restrain it for you, that I may not cut you off. Isaiah 48:9

Do I take any pleasure in the death of the wicked? declares the Lord GOD. Wouldn't I prefer that he turn from his ways and live? Ezekiel 18:23

This is good, and it is pleasing in the sight of God our Savior, who desires all people to be saved and to come to the knowledge of the truth. 1 Timothy 2:3-4

The Lord is not slow in keeping His promise as some understand slowness, but is patient with you, not wanting anyone to perish but everyone to come to repentance. 2 Peter 3:9

I have a question for you. Do you have the courage to endure without quitting? Do you have the courage to endure discrimination, intimidation, and terrorization? Do you have the courage to endure disapproval, dislike, and disparage? Will you suffer through animosity, acrimony, and antagonism? Are you able to suffer through contradiction, disputation, and rejection? Alone you cannot. With God all things are possible. And out of love, long-suffering grows.

Let's talk about gentleness. The very first thing that comes to mind is **Proverbs 15:1. A soft (gentle) answer turns away wrath, but a harsh word stirs up anger.** The verse comes to mind because it is something I have to work at daily. When you exhibit the fruit of gentleness you are kind. You are not harsh but helpful. You are not indifferent but involved. Your words are not piercing but pleasant. You are not condescending but caring.

Therefore welcome one another as Christ has welcomed you, for the glory of God. Romans 15:7

So then, as we have opportunity, let us do good to everyone, and especially to those who are of the household of faith. Galatians 6:10

And the Lord's servant must not be quarrelsome but kind to everyone, able to teach, patiently enduring evil, correcting his opponents with gentleness. God may perhaps grant them repentance leading to a knowledge of the truth, and they may come to their senses and escape from the snare of the devil, after being captured by him to do his will. 2 Timothy 2:24-26

But the wisdom from above is first pure, then peaceable, gentle, open to reason, full of mercy and good fruits, impartial and sincere. James 3:17

But let your adorning be the hidden person of the heart with the imperishable beauty of a gentle and quiet spirit, which in God's sight is very precious. 1 Peter 3:4

Gentleness implies empathy and sympathy. Being kind and forgiving is showing empathy. **(Ephesians 4:32)** Bearing one another's' burdens is an example of this. **(Galatians 6:2)** Affirming others with our words is a display of gentleness. **(Ephesians 4:29)** Counting others as more important than ourselves is another way to show gentleness. **(Philippians 2:3)** If these words do not describe you then there is more work to be done. If you still pick and choose the people you treat this way, it is wrong, and repentance is necessary. There must be more time spent in the Word of God. There should be more time spent in Christ. Abiding in Christ is the key.

We move from gentleness to goodness. What exactly is goodness and who determines if what we are doing is good? Goodness, according to Easton's Bible Dictionary, is not a mere passive quality. It is the firm and persistent resistance of all moral evil, and the choosing and following of all moral good. The only one who can determine this goodness is God. Goodness pours out of a person who knows the value of his or her salvation. This person treats others as they would want them to do unto them. They have a good heart and give unconditionally. They show their love for their enemies through prayer and peacefulness. The person who exhibits goodness does not tolerate letting the people around them treat others wrong. They are not gossipers, backbiters, spiteful, or hateful. They forgive others because they know if they do not God will not forgive them. They take no pleasure in tearing down another person's character. They settle disagreements privately without involving others. This is what God's goodness looks like for us and what our goodness should look like to others.

Oh, taste and see that the LORD is good! Blessed is the man who takes refuge in him! Psalm 34:8

The LORD is good, a stronghold in the day of trouble; he knows those who take refuge in him. Nahum 1:7

The good person out of his good treasure brings forth good, and the evil person out of his evil treasure brings forth evil. Matthew 12:35

Let love be genuine. Abhor what is evil; hold fast to what is good. Romans 12:9

Who is wise and understanding among you? By his good conduct let him show his works in the meekness of wisdom. James 3:13

The last three fruit that overflow from love are faith, meekness, and temperance. The fruit of faith is seen through sacrifice and trusting God in all things. There is no need for revenge because we trust God to fight our battles. The fruit of faith does not doubt God.

And without faith it is impossible to please him, for whoever would draw near to God must believe that he exists and that he rewards those who seek him. Hebrews 11:6

That your faith might not rest in the wisdom of men but in the power of God. 1 Corinthians 2:5

Be watchful, stand firm in the faith, act like men, be strong. 1 Corinthians 16:13

That according to the riches of his glory he may grant you to be strengthened with power through his Spirit in your inner being, so that Christ may dwell in your hearts through faith— that you, being rooted and grounded in love. Ephesians 3:16-17

We are able to obey the commands of God because of our faith in God. We are empowered to walk in the fruit of the Spirit through our faith in God. We embody the fruit of the Spirit and are not afraid to walk by faith because He who promised is faithful. Faith is primarily talked about in relationship to God. Usually we are referring to our belief that God will answer our prayers. I want to challenge you to understand faith also shapes your behaviors.

It is faith in God that makes you pray for your enemies. It is faith in God that makes you bless those who curse you. It is faith in God that makes you turn the other cheek. It is your faith in God that makes you go the extra mile. It is faith in God that makes you do good to those who hate you. It is faith in God that makes us feed our enemies when they are hungry. There should come a time in every Christian's life when you look different than the world. The world does not promote these behaviors, but God does. Who are you looking to please? If you can have faith that God will answer your prayers, then shouldn't you have faith enough to do what He says?

Now that you are familiar with the fruit of faith, let's discuss the fruit of meekness. No one wants to be characterized as weak. We don't want it to appear that anyone is taking advantage of us or getting over on us. Everybody knows that your spouse cheated on you and you are still married. Everybody knows the person who cussed you out and you remained silent. Everybody knows the group of people who are mean to you and talk about you and yet you are kind to them. Everybody knows how you continue to serve the ungrateful. The world would classify all these behaviors as weak. God classifies them as good fruit.

I will never forget the first definition I heard for meekness. Meekness is strength under control. A harnessed horse has not lost its strength; it has gained its usefulness. Story is told of a women's ministry leader who was approached by a very observant new member and asked what she thought about another lady in the church. The young lady was surprised when she only had good things to say about the woman. She said, "Why did you say such good things about someone who treats you so mean?" The leader replied, "You did not ask me what she thought of me. You asked me my opinion of her." This is a classic example of meekness. That is what

I would call a teachable moment. It does not matter what we say, it matters how we live.

Unfortunately, we live in a time where power is pictured as head tall, chest out, leaving everyone around us fearful. You know that pose Superman stands in. This posture signifies don't try me and we think it's cute. It is not. A Christian is powerful when he or she is on bended knee. A Christian is powerful in the posture of humility. A Christian is powerful when he or she takes the unpopular stance. A Christian is powerful when he or she knows where their strength comes from.

But the meek shall inherit the land and delight themselves in abundant peace. Psalm 37:11

"Blessed are the meek, for they shall inherit the earth. Matthew 5:5

Take my yoke upon you, and learn from me, for I am gentle and lowly in heart, and you will find rest for your souls. Matthew 11:29

Finally, brothers, rejoice. Aim for restoration, comfort one another, agree with one another, live in peace; and the God of love and peace will be with you. 2 Corinthians 13:11

See that no one repays anyone evil for evil, but always seek to do good to one another and to everyone. 1 Thessalonians 5:15

A person who bears the fruit of meekness does not care if they are befriended by the popular. He or she would rather have an inclusive group of friends. Meekness frowns on cliques. A person who displays meekness is a friend to all and helps all no matter their status, standing, or situation. There is no taking sides. Meekness helps the suffering. Meekness sees evil and puts a stop to it. The meek person dies to himself or herself every day. The meek person practices self-control. The meek person does not seek revenge, retaliation, or retribution. The meek person offers acceptance and forgiveness to the one who has done the deepest wrong. The meek person knows he or she can do all things through Christ. **(Philippians 4:13)**

The final fruit is temperance. Temperance is synonymous with self-control. Temperance stands against the lust of the flesh, the lust of the eyes, and the pride of life. **(1 John 2:15-16)** A temperate person is intentional. They go beyond changing their physical location. Their intentionality is translated by replacing those things with spiritual disciplines.

Every athlete exercises self-control in all things. They do it to receive a perishable wreath, but we an imperishable.
1 Corinthians 9:25

Older men are to be sober-minded, dignified, self-controlled, sound in faith, in love, and in steadfastness. Titus 2:2

Training us to renounce ungodliness and worldly passions, and to live self-controlled, upright, and godly lives in the present age. Titus 2:12

And knowledge with self-control, and self-control with steadfastness, and steadfastness with godliness. 2 Peter 1:6

Through salvation we become the property and possession of Jesus Christ. The very first step to salvation is acknowledging we are lost and need a Savior. We are tired of living in bondage. We desire to be free. We give up our lives to God. This is not a forced surrender. It is done voluntarily. For this reason, we work out our salvation. For this reason, the Word of God moves from our head to our heart. The fruit of the Spirit are reflected in the details of our lives. Wherever we go, the fruit of the Spirit are shown. We are God's living, breathing, walking, and talking billboards. Walking in the Spirit causes others to want to know Jesus.

"I am crucified with Christ: nevertheless I live; yet not I, but Christ liveth in me: and the life which I now live in the flesh I live by the faith of the Son of God, who loved me, and gave himself for me" Galatians 2:20

"And they that are Christ's have crucified the flesh with the affections and lusts" Galatians 5:24

"For ye are dead, and your life is hid with Christ in God" Col. 3:3

"It is a faithful saying: For if we be dead with him, we shall also live with him" 2 Tim. 2:11

"Who his own self bare our sins in his own body on the tree, that we, being dead to sins, should live unto righteousness: by whose stripes ye were healed" 1 Peter 2:24

Remember when I said we are free. We are free because we are dead. We are dead to the flesh. We no longer live in the place or position of the flesh. This means although we will never be able to live apart from the flesh, we can stop living after the flesh. We desire to follow after righteousness. Following after righteousness means we are led and guided by the Holy Spirit. Walking in the Spirit dictates our conduct, develops our character, and destines us to a complete life in Christ. A life in the Spirit could be described by the lyrics of the late Walker Hawkins' song, What Is This?

What is this
That I feel deep inside
That keeps setting my soul afire
Whatever it is
Whatever it is
Whatever it is
It won't let me
Hold my peace

What is this

That makes people say I'm mad and strange

What is this

That makes me want to run on in Jesus' name

Whatever it is

Whatever it is

Whatever it is

It won't let me

Hold my peace

It makes me love all my enemies

And it makes me love my friends

And it won't let me be ashamed

To tell the world that I've been born again

OOOOH! What is this!

What is this

That makes me do right when I would do wrong

What is this

When I'm down low, it gives me a song

Whatever it is

Whatever it is

Whatever it is

It won't let me

Hold my peace

It makes me love all my enemies

And it makes me love my friends

And it won't let me be ashamed
To tell the world that I've been born again
OOOOH! What is this!

The final question I have for you is are you ready to stop playing a Christian? Are you ready to live up to the name? There comes a time when your only concern is living to please God. Are you ready? Remember you do not have to do it on your own. You have the Holy Spirit to lead, guide, and direct you. You may not be able to live apart from the flesh. You can, however, stop living after the flesh. The choice is yours.

13 A PRAYER FOR SALTED SPEECH

²Continue steadfastly in prayer, being watchful in it with thanksgiving. ³At the same time, pray also for us, that God may open to us a door for the word, to declare the mystery of Christ, on account of which I am in prison— ⁴that I may make it clear, which is how I ought to speak.

⁵Walk in wisdom toward outsiders, making the best use of the time. ⁶Let your speech always be gracious, seasoned with salt, so that you may know how you ought to answer each person. Colossians 4:2-6

I have been privy to many courtroom cases. In the majority of the cases I have observed there is a plaintiff and defendant and two sides are presented before a jury. On occasion, I have witnessed a bench trial. This is a trial where the judge listens to the testimony and decides the fate of the defendant. The wildest thing about bench trials is the words the judge speaks at the end of the testimony. Not only do they pronounce the defendant guilty or not guilty, the judge then calls a recess to determine the defendant's sentencing. If you ever doubted words matter, place yourself in the defendant's seat. This man or woman's entire life is in the hands of someone whose words are the only thing that matters. The words are spoken, and the gavel is banged.

In our text today, Apostle Paul reminds us our words matter. Words spoken without thought and in anger matter. Words spoken in dishonesty matter. Words spoken in haste matter. Words spoken while hurt matter. Words spoken to belittle someone matters. Words spoken to degrade someone matters. All of these are negative ways we can use our words. Paul was personally acquainted with this because he had made a career of persecuting Christians. I imagine he saw the looks on their faces as he attempted to tear down everything they had come to believe. He saw their hurt and helplessness. He saw their anxiety and apprehension. He was a witness to their crying while their beliefs were being crushed.

Now that Paul was playing on God's team, he understood how his words could give hope, help and healing. He wrote letters to the different churches he might enlighten, encourage, and embolden them to stand up for Jesus. So, when he wrote these words to the church of Colossi, his goal was for them to understand the ministry of speech. He began by sharing the highest form of speech every Christian should participate in; praise and worship. I have taught the church I pastor that all prayer should begin with adoration to our God. His name should be elevated before one request is uttered. We must recognize His dominion over heaven and earth and His power to do everything. This principle is taught in Matthew 6 when the disciples ask Jesus to teach them to pray. What were the first words He uttered? Our Father which art in heaven, hallowed be Thy name. What better way to show reverence to our God, acknowledging His worthiness and our unworthiness?

Not only must every child of God honor who God is in prayer, we must also be faithful in prayer. **Continue steadfastly in prayer**, Paul said. **(v.2)** There should never be a time when our prayer life is neglected. There must never be a time when we do not view prayer as a necessity. There must never be time when we do not prostrate ourselves before the Lord because of our needs and the needs of others. Prayer is never selfish. And it is always okay to ask for prayer. A continuous prayer life is evidence of a personal relationship with God. Why else would God tell us in **Philippians 4:6, 1 Thessalonians 5:17 and 1 Timothy 2:1** to continue in prayer.

I love the way Paul demonstrated a faithful prayer life. He also showed us we should be forthright in our prayers. Paul prayed specifically for what he needed. He was jailed because of preaching the Gospel and now asked the church to pray for him that he may be released to continue in this endeavor. He did not pray for words to manipulate the judge so he would be released. He did not use his words to ask them to come and break him out of jail. One thing Paul knew, without a doubt, was there is power in prayer. Paul knew sincere prayer uttered on his behalf to a God who is able to move mountains and open closed doors was more important than appealing to some man or woman here on earth.

I must ask a question. How often do your prayers include an opportunity to lead others to Christ? Are you equipped with the tools to lead someone to Christ? Would you need to call your Pastor, Evangelism leader, or other member of the church if someone said to you, he or she wanted to be saved? There are no chance encounters as children of God. Everyone we come in contact with is sent by God. What would you change if you lived life this way? This is why Paul said pray for me church. He longed for the day of freedom where he could continue to preach and teach the Word of God. He didn't want to be found guilty of preaching coldly, callously, or confusedly. He wanted those he witnessed to hear compassion, caring, and no criticism. Paul knew he could not depend on the anointing from yesterday. He desired a fresh anointing and a rejuvenation of mind, heart, and spirit. Therefore, he reminded the church to continue steadfastly in prayer.

Paul served in Gentile territory. No other place where he was more under scrutiny than there. It is difficult, at times, to live a Christian life with fellow believers. Imagine doing so in front of those whose eyes have been blinded to understand spiritual things. Because they do not understand salvation, forgiveness, grace and mercy, they see every misstep as evidence to their case of why they do not want to become a Christian. Look at the world today. We do not only have believers versus nonbelievers; we have white evangelicals against black preachers. We have those who do not believe Jesus is the Son of God appearing to be more unified than Christians whose lives have been redeemed by the blood of the Lamb. We have members of the same church family against one another. We have unholy talk about the Pastor, his spouse, his family, his staff, and his friends being talked about in mixed company.

Paul knew this day would come and so he admonishes us to walk in wisdom. Remember when Jesus told his disciples to be wise as serpents when he sent them out two by two to witness? **(Matthew 10:16)** Where does this wisdom come from? It most certainly does not come from what we already know. This wisdom comes from God. **(James 1:5)** This wisdom must erase everything we think, what our parents taught us, what other Christians say, and even the findings of world philosophers. The only father that knows best is our heavenly Father. The life we live in the presence of others must be done with integrity and honor. Notice I did not say a perfect life. It should nevertheless, be pleasing in the eyes of the Lord. You do know, **"Godliness is profitable unto all things." 1 Timothy 4:8**

How often do we have good and Godly intentions and then miscarry because our good intentions did not equate to seeking the wisdom of God? How often have we been the carrier of pain instead of peace? How many times have we been messy from misinformation instead of being a missionary of mercy? We are not to bring chaos, clutter, and confusion. We are called to be the carriers of the fruit of the Spirit. This would require sympathy. Not worldly sympathy but Christian sympathy. Sympathy that says, "There, but for the grace of God, there go I." We must remember although we are in the world, we are not of the world. God gives us do overs. However, in the mind of the lost, we get one opportunity to make a first impression for Christ. And this is not just for the unsaved; this is also for the babe in Christ. This is for the one who has endured hard times for a long time and his or her faith is wavering. This is not something to be taken lightly.

Something else we must be sure of in our witness is our calling. We cannot afford to be misdirected. Sometimes you do need to call the Pastor or a stronger believer in Christ. This may have been your assignment instead of speaking earthly wisdom with a hint of Bible. It is never good to share what we think we know. It is always timely to say let me get my Bible or I will get back with you on that issue. If we are angry, this is not the time to speak around other Christians. The words you speak will follow you and you will be held accountable for them. It is not our job to ever influence someone about another human being. Basically, I am saying whether you are struggling with it, stressing over it, or straining just to understand, never speak in haste, hurt, or haughtiness.

Another thing Paul is telling us here is we need to be excited about the Lord. Our lives should be on display for the Lord. They should show the world, the joy and peace we have received from the Lord. When we talk about God, the light that shines should be bright and not dull or dim. When we pray in advance for an opportunity to witness, we should also pray for the exact words to say during the encounter. We should never approach an opportunity to talk about Jesus as a chore. Paul was in jail and yet the excitement and confidence in the words he was writing ooze off the page. He was able to do this because he meditated on the Word of God. He saturated himself in the Word of God. He did not allow his mind to be boggled down with useless information. He was on assignment for the Lord. I know you may be reading this and thinking it's not that serious. Actually, it is. We have no purpose on this earth other than to serve the Lord. We may wear other hats of responsibility. We must remember those hats are secondary to our Christian hat. A good parent, spouse, employee, friend, and church member are an overflow of being a Christian. You cannot be described as good in any of those areas if you are not working on being more like Christ every day. The primary way we do this is by remaining in Christ.

Therefore, if anyone is in Christ, he is a new creation. The old has passed away; behold, the new has come.
2 Corinthians 5:17

For in Christ Jesus you are all sons of God, through faith.
Galatians 3:26

And this is the testimony, that God gave us eternal life, and this life is in his Son. Whoever has the Son has life; whoever does not have the Son of God does not have life. 1 John 5:11-12

Representative Maxine Walters was not the first person to make this next statement. Apostle Paul said it first. When Paul said it, he was telling us make good of every second, minute, hour, day, month and year. Use this time as an opportunity to lift up the name of Jesus. Use this time to do good works. Use this time to tell others about Jesus. Any time is the right time to tell someone Jesus loves them. Anyone who has watched me online knows I do not take for granted everyone watching is saved. This is why I end every broadcast by quoting **John 3:16-17**. Walk in wisdom.

In the book of Ephesians, Paul told us the words we speak should minister grace to those who hear it. We are to let no corrupt talk leave our lips. **(Ephesians 4:29)** Here he takes it one step further, by saying our speech is to be seasoned with salt. **(v.6)** During those times salt was not only used as seasoning, it was also a preservative. It was placed on sacrifices. I wonder what would happen if we looked at every word we speak as a sacrifice to God. We know He is always listening. Or do we? I would imagine if this thought was at the forefront of our minds, we would be more mindful of what we say.

Do you know who was around you when you cussed the cashier while wearing your church t-shirt? Do you know if children were listening when you we gossiping about another member of the church in your kitchen? What about when you are driving down the street and speaking on the phone, who is in the car listening to what you are saying? **Mark 9:50** says, **"Salt is good: but if the salt have lost his saltness, wherewith will ye season it? Have salt in yourselves."**

Unfortunately, too many times we are not very good representatives of Jesus. And the Lord said: **"Because this people draw near with their mouth and honor me with their lips, while** their hearts are far from me, and their fear of me is a commandment taught by men. Isaiah 29:13 When we are rude to others, they may never tell anyone. Guess what? God knows. Death and life are in the power of the tongue, and those who love it will eat its fruits. Proverbs 18:21 When you walk around church so spiritual and then do not speak to another child of God, he or she may not tell a soul. God knows. "'I know your works: you are neither cold nor hot. Would that you were either cold or hot! So, because you are lukewarm, and neither hot nor cold, I will spit you out of my mouth. Revelation 3:15-16. When you are talking on the phone about someone and the individual walks up and does not say anything; do not think you have gotten off the hook. You have not. God knows. For by your words you will be justified, and by your words you will be condemned." Matthew 12:37

We need to take our Christian walk seriously. In this season, people are looking for the real church. They have encountered so many imposters. They are asking, "Will the real Christian stand up? My life is horrible, and I need hope. I have failed so many times, will God forgive me? I am struggling with loving someone who did me wrong, will you pray with me?" We need to stop making excuses for our behavior. What do you think Peter meant when he wrote, **Be ready always to give an answer to every man that asketh you a**

reason of the hope that is in you with meekness and fear. 1 Peter 3:15

Do you always have to react to everything? We are told to walk in meekness. **"Blessed are the meek, for they shall inherit the earth. Matthew 5:5** Anger and arrogance have no room to be on display when we have one focus. How can they reside in you if God is on the throne of your life? **But the meek shall inherit the land and delight themselves in abundant peace. Psalm 37:11** I have said this before. They will know we are Christians by our love. And sometimes we need to realize the lens through which we view certain situations is clouded. Christians have vivid imaginations. We have made imaginary enemies out of people. We cannot shake the fact one person did us wrong, so anyone that comes along has to be the same way. We don't want to deal with our own issues and unhappiness. The Bible says, **"What causes quarrels and what causes fights among you? Is it not this, that your passions are at war within you?" James 4:1**

We walk around giving out counterfeit forgiveness and yet bringing the wrong up every chance we get. Really saints! Do you know why you cannot stand to see others joyful? It is because you have lost your joy. **Therefore be imitators of God, as beloved children. And walk in love, as Christ loved us and gave himself up for us, a fragrant offering and sacrifice to God. Ephesians**

5:1 Do you know why you make up scenarios about other people without proof? It is because you are miserable. Here is a piece of advice. Go find your peace and contentment with life and you will be a better servant of Jesus Christ. **You keep him in perfect peace whose mind is stayed on you, because he trusts in you. Isaiah 26:3**

Bottom line, as Christians we just cannot say everything we are thinking. You cannot take words back. They are out there for eternity. The writer of Hebrews tells us, **Strive for peace with everyone, and for the holiness without which no one will see the Lord. Hebrews 12:14** Another great verse to remember is what speech sounds like to God when not in love. **If I speak in the tongues of men and of angels, but have not love, I am a noisy gong or a clanging cymbal. 1 Corinthians 13:1**

Eddie Murphy starred in the movie, A Thousand Words, as Jack McCall. In the movie, Jack made a living as a literary agent. His success was attributed to saying whatever needed to be said. He is given the assignment to make a deal with a self-help guru. The guru sees right through his falsehoods but agrees to the deal anyway. That night, a Bodhi Tree magically appears in his backyard. Dr. Sinja goes to Jack's house and they both discover for every word that Jack speaks, a leaf will fall off of the tree. When the tree runs out of leaves, the tree will perish, as will Jack. In time, he finds that even written words and gestures count towards his limit; plus, anything that happens to the tree will also affect Jack. When Jack tries to cut it down with an axe, an axe wound appears on him. When squirrels climb the tree, it tickles him. When a gardener tries to poison it with DDT, Jack gets high on the fumes and when the gardener tries to water the tree, Jack starts to sweat/perspire profusely.

His lack of speaking causes miscommunication at work and with his wife, Caroline. Feeling hopeless, he went to the guru and asked what he must do to make things right. He is told to make peace in all of his relationships. At first, he thinks he is referring to his wife. When that didn't work, he visits his mother who tells him she wished he would stop hating his father. He leaves and visits his father's grave and uses his last three words saying, "I forgive you."

Like this character, I have wasted a lot of words. I have used words lying, exaggerating, tearing someone down, and many other things I have said that have no eternal value. And I know I am not by myself. I should have been praying, **Set a guard, O LORD, over my mouth; keep watch over the door of my lips! Psalm 141:3** Another verse I should have been praying was, **Let the words of my mouth and the meditation of my heart be acceptable in your sight, O LORD, my rock and my redeemer. Psalm 19:14** There was a song many years ago entitled, Walk it Out. Paul is telling us, "Don't say it if you cannot back it up. It is more than what you say, it is also about what you do. **If you really fulfill the royal law according to the Scripture, "You shall love your neighbor as yourself," you are doing well. James 2:8**

When your walk does not walk in step with your talk, it is silenced. You are speaking and it has no earthly value. Many tables in the fellowship hall and conversations after church would cease to exist if our speech wasn't edifying to others. Truth be told, some of the people in your circle are only there because you always have something messy to say. Your only reason for having social media accounts is to find out the business of others. You don't like, share, or comment on anything on their pages. You unfriend or block people only to watch what they post from someone else's account. And in this season, people are questioning why we are in the midst of a global pandemic, looking for the next year to be better, and yet we are still the same.

I must pause before I end this day by asking what do your nonverbal communications reflect? Is your social media timeline seasoned with salt? May I inquire also about your text messages, and direct messages? Sometimes it is not about what you speak, it is about what you type. **If anyone thinks he is religious and does not bridle his tongue but deceives his heart, this person's religion is worthless. James 1:26** Are you edifying saints and lifting up the name of Jesus? I regularly joke with my members about how they post everything on their timelines except that which lifts up Jesus. I can't get them to share things from our church. It makes me wonder if the friends they have don't know they are Christians. They may be known for attending church, but do their lives outside of church reflect accepting the Savior? Are they known more for their worldly behaviors instead of the transformed life God has granted them to possess? **Put on then, as God's chosen ones, holy and beloved, compassionate hearts, kindness, humility, meekness, and patience, bearing with one another and, if one has a complaint against another, forgiving each other; as the Lord has forgiven you, so you also must forgive. And above all these put on love, which binds everything together in perfect harmony. Colossians 3:12-14**

I have said a lot in these few pages. Some of you may have stopped reading because you felt like you were being picked on. You were not. Be grateful for that feeling. It is the Holy Spirit telling you something needs to change in your life. Some of you may have read to the end thinking, Pastor G is not talking to me. Yes, I was. We all stand in need of improvement. We are being sanctified. This means this makeover process is continuous. It only ends at death. Hatred is spreading like wildflowers. Racism is at an all-time high. It does not matter when you read this book, in 2021 or many years later, the problems will be the same because the root cause is sin. Paul tells us in Romans, **¹⁷ Repay no one evil for evil, but give thought to do what is honorable in the sight of all. ¹⁸ If possible, so far as it depends on you, live peaceably with all. ¹⁹ Beloved, never avenge yourselves, but leave it to the wrath of God, for it is written, "Vengeance is mine, I will repay, says the Lord." ²⁰ To the contrary, "if your enemy is hungry, feed him; if he is thirsty, give him something to drink; for by so doing you will heap burning coals on his head." ²¹ Do not be overcome by evil, but overcome evil with good. Romans 12:17-21**

Why don't you make a promise to God today to be a part of the solution? Stop pretending and start walking it out. **Through him then let us continually offer up a sacrifice of praise to God, that is, the fruit of lips that acknowledge his name. Do not neglect to do good and to share what you have, for such sacrifices are pleasing to God. Hebrews 13:15-16** Being a Christian is not about how you feel. Being a Christian is really about doing what Jesus would do. Only a totally surrendered life to Christ can walk this out. **But be doers of the word, and not hearers only, deceiving yourselves. James 1:22**

14 A PRAYER TO BE EQUIPPED

Now may the God of peace who brought again from the dead our Lord Jesus, the great shepherd of the sheep, by the blood of the eternal covenant, [21] equip you with everything good that you may do his will, working in us that which is pleasing in his sight, through Jesus Christ, to whom be glory forever and ever. Amen. Hebrews 13:20-21

Perfection. By definition this word means the condition, state, or quality of being free or as free as possible from all flaws or defects. The question I want to pose to you today is; are there any perfect people? The good Christian answer is only Jesus was perfect. Then why do we act as though we are perfect? I know we think we do not. The truth is every time we stand with fake faultlessness in judgment of others we are walking in pretend perfection. We say the Bible says there is none righteous, no not one, and yet once we have been saved for a while and don't do some of the things we used to do, we forget this fact.

In this doxology, the writer of Hebrews is telling us there is only one way to be made perfect. This act can only be done by the God of peace. Let's take a look at this phrase "make you perfect". Take note that the audience to which this was wrote each had their own understanding of what this word meant. The doctors of that time understood it to mean setting a broken bone. The fisherman understood it to mean mending a net. Soldiers understood it to mean equipping them for battle and the sailor understood it to mean outfitting the ship to sail.

You are probably reading this saying what does any of this have to do with me. Our survival on this earth is dependent upon what we receive from God. God wants to take our brokenness and help us walk uprightly. He is the only One who can do it because He is the only perfect being. He is also the only One who knows the true purpose we were created for. God wants us to be able to run our races with perseverance. We all have been given the assignment to catch fish. Before we can do that God has to mend the breaks in our nets. This is the only way we will be able to win souls for Him. This life we live will not be easy. Storms will come our way. It is God who equips us for battle so we will not end up battered by every storm we face. For God to make us perfect, He must grow us up.

2 Timothy 3:16-17 tells us one of the ways God matures us. It says, [16] **All Scripture is breathed out by God and profitable for teaching, for reproof, for correction, and for training in righteousness,** [17] **that the man of God may be complete, equipped for every good work.** We cannot complete the work of saving souls without correct doctrine. This is reproof. The only place this doctrine is proven to be true is the Holy Bible. This is the only book written back by the authority of God. Yes, there are commentaries, books, sermons, and teachings written by men. These things should only be looked at as add-ons to the Word of God. They should never be replacements for prayerful study of the Word of God.

The second purpose of the Word of God is correcting our error in judgment. Believe it or not, this is easier to do from those who have lived an outwardly sinful life. It is more difficult for those who believe they have lived a pretty good life. They believe they have not committed the really bad sins. These individuals have a hard time accepting the fact they need a Savior. They read the Bible, listen to sermons with a preconceived notion of what is right and what is wrong. These are the individuals who listen the entire time thinking about the people they need to share the sermon with because it was for them. It is important for us to remember we are all depraved, weak and unable to live a righteous life alone. We need God.

Whoever loves discipline loves knowledge, but he who hates reproof is stupid. Proverbs 12:1

Whoever ignores instruction despises himself, but he who listens to reproof gains intelligence. Proverbs 15:32

My brothers, if anyone among you wanders from the truth and someone brings him back, let him know that whoever brings back a sinner from his wandering will save his soul from death and will cover a multitude of sins. James 5:19-20

The third purpose of the Word of God is correction. We can live our entire life doing something one way. An example of this is driving. We typically drive in the same manner of the person who taught us. Drivers' education was not required as it is now. When I was growing up it was only an incentive to get a discount on automobile insurance. Depending on our teachers we did not learn all the legal rules to driving. The lack of knowledge causes us to fail the driving test the first time. It is only after we are taught the correct way to drive and actually put it into practice are, we able to pass the test. Come closer children. We were all raised a certain way. Some of us were raised in Christian homes and some were not. We are products of whoever had the biggest influence over our lives. Unfortunately, the way in which we were raised coupled with the ways of the world taint our beliefs and behaviors. We must read the Word of God with a clear head and open heart. We must prepare or cultivate our hearts to hear when something we are doing or have done needs to be corrected. We may not be able to trust another imperfect being; however, when we read it for ourselves, we can trust God. The choice then becomes ours to change.

The final purpose of the Word of God is instruction in righteousness. God does not expect us to figure this thing out all by ourselves. There is a verse in the Bible for every situation. God wants us to love the Word. **Psalm 119:162** says, **I rejoice at thy word, as one that findeth great spoil**. Verse 167 says, **My soul hath observed thy testimonies; and I love them exceedingly.** Verse 67 says, **Before I was afflicted I went astray; but now I observe thy word.** There is sufficiency in Scripture. Christians do not have to look elsewhere for answers to life's challenges. Yet, we do. And this is precisely the reason so many of us remain babes in Christ.

"Behold, blessed is the one whom God reproves; therefore despise not the discipline of the Almighty. Job 5:17

For whatever was written in former days was written for our instruction, that through endurance and through the encouragement of the Scriptures we might have hope. Romans 15:4

Pastor F. Bernard Mitchell, Pastor of Zion Hill Baptist Church in Mendenhall, Mississippi said, "It is not enough for a Christian to know and quote the Scripture. He or she must believe and receive it." Spiritual maturity takes discipline. This is not the discipline of attending church, serving meals to the homeless, singing in the choir, teaching Sunday School, or standing on the door. This is the discipline of studying the Word of God daily. The discipline required is memorizing and meditating on Scripture. This is one of the ways to katartidzo. Katartidzo is the Greek word for "to make perfect".

Another way we are made perfect is through prayer. It has been said that we will never graduate from the school of faith. Like the church at Thessalonica, our faith is defective. (cf. **2 Thessalonians 3:10**) Our lack of knowledge can be decreased through the reading of the Word. Our reading of the Word of God must be coupled with prayer. I must say it again. We live in a sinful world. We are saved by grace through faith. Our faith starts out weak. As we follow the instructions given in **2 Peter 1:5-6,** our faith grows and is strengthened as our spiritual knowledge grows. But notice, even those who far surpass others in their faith walk are still lacking. It is imperative in our Christian journey to always keep our deficiencies in view. This will keep us from becoming stagnant. Remember Paul said to forget what lies behind and keep pressing toward the mark. **(Philippians 3:13-14)** Here are just a few more verses to support the need for continuous prayer.

Rejoice in hope, be patient in tribulation, be constant in prayer. Romans 12:12

Pray without ceasing. 1 Thessalonians 5:17

Praying at all times in the Spirit, with all prayer and supplication. To that end keep alert with all perseverance, making supplication for all the saints. Ephesians 6:18

Continue steadfastly in prayer, being watchful in it with thanksgiving. Colossians 4:2

In every book I have written I am aware I will have a few skeptics. There is someone, I suspect, reading this who is asking, why didn't God just make us perfect? There is probably someone else asking, if God does not expect us to be perfect, then why the emphasis on perfection. Allow me to address the first question. If God where to create another perfect being, He would simply be creating Himself. He, instead, created humans He could love and would love Him in return. When we are made aware of the many ways God demonstrated and continues to demonstrate His love for us, should we not love Him in return? Our obedience to God is evidence of our love for Him. God did not want a bunch of robots.

Think about what **Philippians 2:5-7** says. **⁵Have this mind among yourselves, which is yours in Christ Jesus, ⁶who, though he was in the form of God, did not count equality with God a thing to be grasped, ⁷but emptied himself, by taking the form of a servant, being born in the likeness of men.** Since Jesus considered equality unattainable, shouldn't we? Jesus sacrificed His life for you and me. He who knew no sin became sin. Yes, He was still one hundred percent man. Yet, He made Himself a little lower than the angels. I often think to myself why I would ever be disobedient to One who sacrificed so much. The closest person who came close to this kind of sacrifice for me was my dearly beloved mother, Queen Cleopatra. I am also blessed to see the way my wife, Janice, gives selflessly in the care of her sister and our grandchildren. Even with all the sacrifices they make, they still do not come close to the sacrifice Jesus, our elder brother, made for us.

I want to take the focus off perfection for a while. Too often when we focus on perfection, we set our actions and attitudes on accomplishing something. I kept that rule. I didn't break that one. Paul is trying to teach us here in the book of Colossians that it is

God who does the perfecting. The more we surrender to Him, the more natural it becomes. It is like learning how to ride a bicycle. Your dad or big brother is always there behind you holding you up. Eventually, he lets go. He continues to follow you even though you are riding on your own. Jesus did not leave us comfortless. The more we yield to the Holy Spirit the more we become more like Christ. When we are more like Christ, the more our behaviors reflect the fruit of the Spirit.

The final two ways we are being perfected is by the saints and through suffering. I tell all young preachers, don't do ministry alone. You need someone walking with you. You need that person who will correct you in love. You need that person who will stay beside you even when you mess up. You need someone who you can be honest and say I am really not doing good right now. I need you to pray for me. I need your encouragement. And the important thing about this is even if you don't have that person(s) right now; you can pray and ask God to send you that person. **"For where two or three are gathered in my name, there am I among them." Matthew 18:20** I chose to put shouldering and suffering together because it is the same individual(s) who lend you their shoulder that will walk with you through suffering. These individuals will remind you suffering is for your benefit. It is also our responsibility to make sure the church does not die with us. God has not taken us through all we have gone through only for ourselves. Just as the Scriptures were written for our benefit, our suffering is experienced to bless somebody else.

Today I am reminded that prayer is essential for us to be made perfect. And while this is a prayer for today, I would encourage you to make this a daily prayer. "Lord sanctify me in Your truth. I ask You to continue to make me perfect through the modes and mediums You see fit. Not my will, but Thy will be done. In Jesus' name amen."

15 A PRAYER AGAINST SPIRITUAL BLINDNESS

⁶Humble yourselves, therefore, under the mighty hand of God so that at the proper time he may exalt you, ⁷casting all your anxieties on him, because he cares for you. ⁸Be sober-minded; be watchful. Your adversary the devil prowls around like a roaring lion, seeking someone to devour. ⁹Resist him, firm in your faith, knowing that the same kinds of suffering are being experienced by your brotherhood throughout the world. ¹⁰And after you have suffered a little while, the God of all grace, who has called you to his eternal glory in Christ, will himself restore, confirm, strengthen, and establish you. ¹¹To him be the dominion forever and ever. Amen. 1 Peter 5:6-11

Humility. What the world needs more of. I know the song says the world needs more love. I would, however, beg to differ. Humility requires one to realize he or she cannot make it on their own. One who is humble knows it is not their bloodline, neighborhood, possessions, education, or associates that has caused them to be successful. A person who is humble measures success by how much he or she can do for God. Look around on the news, on social media, on the worldwide web and what to you see. You see people praising themselves or other people praising them.

Do you know what one of the major differences between the church of today and the church of yesterday? The members of the congregations depending solely on God. If they received something, they thanked God for it. It was not about the money or the job they had. God was the source of everything. It is this kind of thinking so many of us have moved away from and the world is suffering for it. There is a lack of humility. Everyone appears to be worried about making their name great. I hear a lot of talk about leaving a legacy. I contend, if the legacy is not attached to knowing who Jesus is and how to pray, it is worthless.

Apostle Peter begins verse 6 by saying, **⁶ Humble yourselves, therefore, under the mighty hand of God so that at the proper time he may exalt you.** Peter understood how easy it would be to believe the hype. Peter was the one who preached and five thousand were saved and then another three thousand. Peter the Pastor of the New Testament church. I am sure he heard the people's praises because of the things he was able to do in the name of Jesus. It would have been very easy for him to get puffed up. However, Peter did not. He walked with Jesus and saw how Jesus lived. He saw how he responded after feeding the five thousand and healing the blind man. He saw how He sent the onlookers away before He resurrected Lazarus and Jairus' daughter. It was never about Him. It was always about doing the will of His Father. Peter had the best example and wanted to share this example with all of us.

Notice the therefore in the middle of verse six. If you have been around me anytime you know I always say when you see the word therefore, you must ask what it is there for. In this case, the answer is in verse 5, where Peter tells us, **God opposes the proud but gives grace to the humble."** When we are prideful, we are in direct opposition with God. When we are prideful both our witness and testimony are ruined. This is why he said clothe yourselves. In the Greek, this phrase means to tie yourself up in humility. Gather it around you and tie it tight so that the wind and the rain cannot cause it to fall off. Peter was saying, the people should not notice your eloquent speech, how you can draw a crowd, how many disciples you have or even the four-piece suit or the red bottoms that adorn your feet. The first thing people should notice about us is our humility.

I want to take this one step further because in those times there was a cape worn by the slaves to indicate their submissiveness to their master. This is the perfect picture I want you to see today. The humility we should be clothed with also signifies our submissiveness to God. It declared their attitude of service. It was not forced on the slave. The slave wore it willingly and with a sense of pride. Pride that said I am excited, elated, ecstatic to serve my master. Isn't this how we should be when serving God?

Let me pause for a moment and ask you a question. Have you lost your joy in serving the Lord? Has the waiting room become the whining room? Have you disrobed humility and picked up a hustle? Do you appease God for the approval of the saints? Have you become a victim to the "God needs some help" crowd? What is the foundation for your service to the Lord? Does it appear your dream has been deferred and God has disappointed you?

Back to the text. Once we are clothed in humility, God then sends affliction our way. What better time than for your faith to be proven than in affliction and adversity! These are the times when we must trust God to lift us up out of the sad and lowly state. This is the time when our minds must be focused on God to ensure our peace. The lifting we are waiting for does not occur when we want it to. It occurs at the right time which only God knows. It may be a lifting now or a lifting in the life to come. The takeaway for this moment is we must wait on God's timing. Self-elevated people often become the commercial for what life looks like without God. In the lives of self-elevated people there is no joy and no peace in what they are doing. Service for God seems like a chore. It is treated as an inconvenience. My advice to you today is wait for God to do it!

The reward for humility and fear of the LORD is riches and honor and life. Proverbs 22:4

He has told you, O man, what is good; and what does the LORD require of you but to do justice, and to love kindness, and to walk humbly with your God? Micah 6:8

But he gives more grace. Therefore it says, "God opposes the proud, but gives grace to the humble." James 4:6

During the time of waiting it may appear your burdens become heavier. I have often found myself in the ministry God gave me wondering why it has not yet brought forth the financial blessing God promised me when He gave the vision. It is this verse that always reminds me, it is not the right time. And I continue to put pen to paper writing books and praying for pastors. I do it not because I have received an earthly prize but because I know my obedience will yield an eternal weight in glory. I do this in the midst of those who may not understand my dedication nor my diligence. I also do it because of the next verse. Verse 7 says, **casting all your anxieties on him, because he cares for you.**

Anxiety stems from a lack of confidence in God. Anxiety comes from a disagreement in the mind. On one hand we read God's promises for us and on the other hand we see our current situation before us. Anxiety is thinking we could better manage our lives on our own without interference from God. After all, it appears God is who is causing the hold up. I could be further along if God wouldn't have let my parent die in the middle of my college studies. I would be better off if God had not given me a bad spouse, making me a single parent. I would be better off if I didn't tithe. I would be better off if I aligned myself with someone, I know God has shown me was no good for me. Anxiety comes from thinking God is wrong.

When I am afraid, I put my trust in you. Psalm 56:3
When the cares of my heart are many, your consolations cheer my soul. Psalm 94:19

So, Pastor Peter tells us while we are waiting on God, trust He knows best for us, He is not going to leave us carrying the weight. God loves us and cares for us. He is not inflicting the hurt to harm us. It is inflicted to produce devotion, dedication, and to death do us part. It is inflicted so that when the next situation occurs, we will look at God's track record in our lives and remember He has always answered our prayers. No matter how dark the night or disappointing the day, God has been there. And His presence should provide the assurance we can cast our family cares, financial cares, health cares, cares for the present and cares for the future on Him. Why? Because the Scripture tells us He who promised is faithful. **(Hebrews 10:23)** In fact, He is faithful even when we are faithless. **(2 Timothy 2:13)** Who wouldn't trust a God like this? Unfortunately, and all too often, we don't.

" Love Is a Battlefield " is a song by American singer Pat Benatar, released on September 12, 1983, as a single from Benatar's live album Live from Earth (1983). This song was penned by Holly Knight and Mike Chatman. It was ranked as number 30 in the Top 100 songs of 1980. I didn't tell you this for you to start singing the song. I am telling you this to remind you, life is a battlefield. Every day we are engaged in spiritual warfare, whether we choose to participate or not. Our alignment with God made us an enemy of Satan. And whether or not we choose to acknowledge it and arm ourselves with the spiritual weapons of our warfare which are mighty in God, we will feel defeated.

Burdens distract us. They cause us to disengage from our primary purpose. Burdens disallow the power of God to be seen in our lives. Now if pleasing God is not your primary purpose then keep carrying your own burdens. I feel though someone maybe even two or three of the people reading this may be tired of trying to do it on their own. You realize you cannot fix your marriage. You realize you can't mend that friendship. You have tried everything else, so why not try it God's way? Even if you do not decide to take your burden to the Lord and leave it there, the target is still on your back. The enemy has not taken his eyes off you. His goal is now and will always be to devour you. He does not only want to knock you down; he wants to take you out. He wants to render you incapacitated and unable to stand and be the light of the world. His goal never changes. You may think through observation that his focus is on somebody else and he has forgotten you. He has not. Let me say that again. He has not. He is still seeking you out. And if he is not, then it is because you are making no impact for the kingdom of God.

Let me share a few Scriptures with you.

"Yet the Lord thinketh on me," was the consolation of David, when he felt that he was "poor and needy," Psalm 40:17.

But if God so clothes the grass of the field, which today is alive and tomorrow is thrown into the oven, will he not much more clothe you, O you of little faith? [31] Therefore do not be anxious, saying, 'What shall we eat?' or 'What shall we drink?' or 'What shall we wear?' [32] For the Gentiles seek after all these things, and your heavenly Father knows that you need them all. Matthew 6:30-32

"Can a woman forget her nursing child, that she should have no compassion on the son of her womb? Even these may forget, yet I will not forget you. Isaiah 49:15

Humble submission is attached to confident reliance on the goodness of God. Humble submission exempts us from care. We should all pray for a heart of humility. Our prayers should include total submission to God. We must pray and ask God to help us to release expectations from the people around us to carry our burdens. We must release the burden from our spouses, parents, friends, pastors, etc. to fix our problems. We must ask God for the freedom from carrying our own burden to please everyone and make them happy. When Pastor Peter says cast your anxieties on the Lord, he means everything. We do ourselves a disservice depending on other people to fix our broken hearts, fight our battles, and take care of us. Our God is near the brokenhearted and saves the crushed in spirit. **(Psalm 34:18)** This battle is not ours but the Lords. **(2 Chronicles 20:15)** God cares for us. **(1 Peter 5:7)**

Just as there is nothing new under the sun, you are not the only one suffering. You are not the only one experiencing tests and trials. Verse 8 warned us of an enemy who is out to get us. **John 10:10** tells us this same enemy comes to steal, kill, and destroy. Since his attacks are imminent, be prepared. Know he is not going to come without force and with the very things you desire, so you must resist him. How do you resist him? You resist him by not backing down and standing up to him. This does not mean sit back and let things take its course. This means use the sword of the spirit and fight the good fight of faith.

Some of you reading this are members of a fraternity or sorority. There were rituals every member participated in to become a member. No matter where you go there are things that identify you as a member. It may be a piece of clothing or jewelry. It may be a song or a pledge. When you don't know these things, your membership is questioned. Pastor Peter tells us in verse 9, as Christians we are members of a group. Our faith identifies us as a member. We are all to respond the same way and encourage one another as they go through suffering. There should be a mutual front against the enemy. **1 Corinthians 10:13** is another verse that illustrates the fraternal order of suffering for those who are met at the foot of the cross acknowledging we were sinners. And if that does not bring you consolation, ponder the fact our elder brother, Jesus, went first. While we were at the foot of the cross, He was on the cross.

There is nevertheless a predetermined purpose for the suffering. **Romans 5:3-5** and **James 1:2-4** give us an earlier picture of the significance of suffering. Suffering is not payback for our sins.

Suffering is not done so God and Jesus and sit up and brag on how they did this and that. They are not taking bets on who will pass and who will fail. No, we were left with all the tools needed to pass the tests we are given. In Romans, suffering produces patience and patience character and character hope. In James, trials bring about patience and patience must have its full effect (run its complete course) so we will be mature not lacking anything. And now here in 1 Peter 5, we have another positive result from suffering.

Pastor Peter is saying because of what suffering produces, time should not be a factor. If we are going to be shaped into the image of Jesus Christ, we must suffer. Notice the word will or shall in the King James Version. Shall was a strengthened form of not yet but with certainty. The word shall implies an authority behind the verb mentioned to make it happen. Let me give you a few examples just in case you are one of the ones who need additional proof.

So shall my word be that goes out from my mouth; it shall not return to me empty, but it shall accomplish that which I purpose, and shall succeed in the thing for which I sent it.

Isaiah 55:11

Blessed are the pure in heart, for they shall see God.

Matthew 5:8

Blessed are the peacemakers, for they shall be called sons of God. Matthew 5:9

And I give unto them eternal life; and they shall never perish, neither shall any man pluck them out of my hand.
John 10:28 KJV

And whatsoever ye shall ask in my name, that will I do, that the Father may be glorified in the Son. John 14:13 KJV

Behold! I tell you a mystery. We shall not all sleep, but we shall all be changed, [52] in a moment, in the twinkling of an eye, at the last trumpet sound, and the dead will be raised imperishable, and we shall all be changed.   1
11 Corinthians 15:51-52

This I say then, Walk in the Spirit, and ye shall not fulfil the lust of the flesh. Galatians 5:16 KJV

There are many more Scriptures which point to the authority of God. I would recommend you take some time to search the Scriptures for yourself. These verses will serve as a good resource to resist the devil.

I want to take a look, now, at the individual results of suffering mentioned in verse 10. The first word is restore. The KJV says, 'make you perfect'. This refers to us not having any defect in us. Picture having a bone or joint out of place and the doctor putting it back in place. In this case, we have the Great Physician; adjusting the defects we inherited though birth and restoring us to the form God created us to have from the beginning of time. The word confirm, signifies attaching us to Himself so that we will be steadfast and solid. We will be immovable. The word strengthen, refers to being able to withstand any force. We will receive enormous strength that only comes from God. **Ephesians 3:16** says, **that according to the riches of his glory he may grant you to be strengthened with power through his Spirit in your inner being.** The final word establish, refers to our foundation. Pastor Peter is saying because of our sufferings, we will be like the little pig who made his house of bricks, no matter the severity of the storm, we will continue to stand. Only God can settle our nerves, thoughts, insecurities, and fears. Our part is to draw near to God as we endure suffering. The Bible says, **"Everyone then who hears these words of mine and does them will be like a wise man who built his house on the rock. [25] And the rain fell, and the floods came, and the winds blew and beat on that house, but it did not fall, because it has been founded on the rock." (Matthew 7:24-25).**

Child of God, this is good news. The news is so good that in the final verse Pastor Peter bursts out in praise. He was in awe of the ability of God. He was in amazement of the authority of God. He stood in admiration of the authenticity of God. He had that ah-ha moment of all God really does for us. He saves us. **(John 3:16)** He seals us. **(2 Corinthians 1:22)**. He secures our salvation. **(John 10:27-30)** He satisfies us. **(Psalm 22:26)**.   He sanctified us. **(Hebrews 10:10)** He strengthens us. **(Philippians 4:13)** He supplies us with sufficient grace. **(2 Corinthians 12:9)** He speaks to us. **(Romans 15:4)** He sustains us. **(Psalm 54:4)** What can you add to the list? What has He done specifically for you? Was it such that you would pause right now and burst out in praise at the very thought of it? If you didn't, you should. I know without a doubt God has been good to you. Because our God does not change. God can be trusted.

We can depend on God. He can make something out of nothing. He can heal, deliver, restore, forgive, resurrect, pardon, redeem, justify, sanctify, and will glorify. Do you get the picture? Has the thought been solidified in your mind? If you desire God to exalt you, you must clothe yourself in humility. You must cast all your cares upon the Lord with confidence. There should be no pity parties in the body of Christ because we all suffer. Stay on alert. Don't have your mind all boggled down with unnecessary things. Keep your mind clear to receive directions from God. You must resist the devil and stand firm in your faith. You need to walk around with God confidence at all times. And finally, don't wait to praise God after He does it. Praise Him simply because He can.

ABOUT THE AUTHOR

Teron V. Gaddis is the founder of Pastor G Ministries. He is the current pastor of Greater Bethel Church in Oklahoma City, OK. Pastor G (as he is affectionately called) has been in the ministry for 37 years and pastoring for 29 years. He is married to Janice for thirty-four years and together they have 5 children and 11 grandchildren. Pastor G is known for his biblical preaching and teaching with soul-stirring illustrations that make his Bible studies and sermons understandable for both the young and old. Pastor G Ministries was birthed because of his heart for Pastors. In 2014, he added the ministry, **"Praying for our Pastors"**. The purpose and goal of P4OP is to cover every Pastor in prayer and to teach congregations the importance of praying the Word of God over their Pastors. Our heart's desire is for "no Pastor to be left behind". Through the Word of God, we want to 'change lives one verse at a time'.

Additional resources by Teron V. Gaddis

Praying for our Pastors

WE WIN 31-Day Devotional

WE WIN: 31-Day Devotional & Small Group Study

Powerful Prayers for All Seasons: Old Testament

TSI: The Servant's Identity

Pastor G Ministries would like to make a personal appeal to you. If you have a heart for Pastors and believe in the power of prayer, our ministry is for you.

Text "prayer" to (405) 622-8448.

If you are a Pastor and would like for us to pray for you, text "Pastor" to (405) 622-8448.

For more information about Praying for Pastors:
Pastor G Ministries
Post Office 1083
Oklahoma City, OK 73101
(405) 657-4463

Made in the USA
Middletown, DE
17 April 2022

64386923R00137